Italian and Italian American Studies

Series Editor: **Stanislao G. Pugliese**, Hofstra University

This publishing initiative seeks to bring the latest scholarship in Italian and Italian American history, literature, cinema, and cultural studies to a large audience of specialists, general readers, and students. I&IAS will feature works on modern Italy (Renaissance to the present) and Italian American culture and society by established scholars as well as new voices in the academy. This endeavor will help to shape the evolving fields of Italian and Italian American Studies by re-emphasizing the connection between the two. The following editorial board consists of esteemed senior scholars who act as advisors to the series editor.

REBECCA WEST
University of Chicago

FRED GARDAPHÉ
Queens College, CUNY

ALESSANDRO PORTELLI
Università di Roma "La Sapienza"

JOSEPHINE GATTUSO HENDIN
New York University

PHILIP V. CANNISTRARO[†]
Queens College and the Graduate School, CUNY

Titles include:

Nicoletta Pireddu
THE WORKS OF CLAUDIO MAGRIS
Temporary Homes, Mobile Identities, European Borders

Simona Frasca
ITALIAN BIRDS OF PASSAGE
The Diaspora of Neapolitan Musicians in New York

Deborah Amberson and Elena Past (*editors*)
THINKING ITALIAN ANIMALS
Human and Posthuman in Modern Italian Literature and Film

Lorenzo Benadusi and Giorgio Caravale (*editors*)
GEORGE L. MOSSE'S ITALY
Interpretation, Reception, and Intellectual Heritage

Giovanni Orsina
BERLUSCONISM AND ITALY: A HISTORICAL INTERPRETATION

Stefania Lucamante
FORGING SHOAH MEMORIES
Italian Women Writers, Jewish Identity, and the Holocaust

Maristella Cantini (*editor*)
ITALIAN WOMEN FILMMAKERS AND THE GENDERED SCREEN

Norma Bouchard and Valerio Ferme
ITALY AND THE MEDITERRANEAN
Words, Sounds, and Images of the Post-Cold War Era

Amedeo Osti Guerrazzi, translated by Elizabeth Burke and Anthony Majanlahti
THE ITALIAN ARMY IN SLOVENIA
Strategies of Antipartisan Repression, 1941–1943

Ruth Glynn
WOMEN, TERRORISM AND TRAUMA IN ITALIAN CULTURE
The Double Wound

Cristina Lombardi-Diop and Caterina Romeo (*editors*)
POSTCOLONIAL ITALY
The Colonial Past in Contemporary Culture

Giovanna Faleschini Lerner
CARLO LEVI'S VISUAL POETICS
The Painter as Writer

Giulia Albanese and Roberta Pergher (*editors*)
IN THE SOCIETY OF FASCISTS
Acclamation, Acquiescence, and Agency in Mussolini's Italy

Paolo Pezzino, translated by Noor Giovanni Mazhar
MEMORY AND MASSACRE
Revisiting Sant'Anna di Stazzema

Sebastian Fichera
ITALY ON THE PACIFIC
San Francisco's Italian Americans

Risa Sodi and Millicent Marcus (*editors*)
NEW REFLECTIONS ON PRIMO LEVI
Before and After Auschwitz

Philip Cooke
THE LEGACY OF THE ITALIAN RESISTANCE

Mahnaz Yousefzadeh
CITY AND NATION IN THE ITALIAN UNIFICATION
The National Festivals of Dante Alighieri

Angelo Del Boca; translated by Antony Shugaar
MOHAMED FEKINI AND THE FIGHT TO FREE LIBYA

Thomas Simpson
MURDER AND MEDIA IN THE NEW ROME
The Fadda Affair

William J. Connell and Fred Gardaphé (*editors*)
ANTI-ITALIANISM
Essays on a Prejudice

Cristina M. Bettin
ITALIAN JEWS FROM EMANCIPATION TO THE RACIAL LAWS

palgrave▶pivot

The Works of Claudio Magris: Temporary Homes, Mobile Identities, European Borders

Nicoletta Pireddu

palgrave
macmillan

THE WORKS OF CLAUDIO MAGRIS
Copyright © Nicoletta Pireddu, 2015.

All rights reserved.

First published in 2015 by
PALGRAVE MACMILLAN®
in the United States—a division of St. Martin's Press LLC,
175 Fifth Avenue, New York, NY 10010.

Where this book is distributed in the UK, Europe and the rest of the world, this is by Palgrave Macmillan, a division of Macmillan Publishers Limited, registered in England, company number 785998, of Houndmills, Basingstoke, Hampshire RG21 6XS.

Palgrave Macmillan is the global academic imprint of the above companies and has companies and representatives throughout the world.

Palgrave® and Macmillan® are registered trademarks in the United States, the United Kingdom, Europe and other countries.

ISBN: 978–1–137–48802–2 EPUB
ISBN: 978–1–137–48804–6 PDF
ISBN: 978–1–137–49262–3 Hardback

Library of Congress Cataloging-in-Publication Data is available from the Library of Congress.

A catalogue record of the book is available from the British Library.

First edition: 2015

www.palgrave.com/pivot

DOI: 10.1057/9781137488046

A Claudio Magris

Contents

Preface   viii

Introduction   1
    Claudio Magris's geography of domesticity   2

1   Households of the Self   10
    1.1   *Stadelmann*: dwelling in the space of the "-ex"   11
    1.2   At the self's door: *You Will Therefore Understand* and *Voices*   18
    1.3   Hosting life in the moment: *A Different Sea* and *Il Conde*   24

2   Homely Memories, Promised Homelands   32
    2.1   A nomad and fugitive abode: Trieste and its narratives   33
    2.2   *Inferences from a Sabre*: mapping the heart's homestead   42

3   European Thresholds and Relocations   51
    3.1   Mitteleuropa: a dislodged center   52
    3.2   *Danube*: the liquid path to rooted homelessness   57
       3.2.1   Fluctuating domiciles   58
       3.2.2   Soluble sites   62
       3.2.3   House, town, community   66
       3.2.4   Flowing home?   71

4   From Snug Refuges to Ghastly Cells   76
    4.1   *Microcosms*: the *flâneur* in his homescapes   77
       4.1.1   Image masonry   77

	4.1.2 Domestic aromas	80
	4.1.3 Residential antinomies	86
4.2	Global unhomeliness: *Blindly*	91
5	**Habitat and Habitus**	**102**
5.1	The essayist and the tortoise	103
5.2	Edifices of values	107
5.3	The fortress and the drawbridge	116

Conclusion	123
Bibliography	127
Index	135

Preface

The idea for this project was born when I delved into Claudio Magris's *Danubio* [*Danube*] in the framework of my wider research on the European consciousness in literature sponsored by the National Endowment for the Humanities and the George A. and Eliza Gardner Howard Foundation at Brown University. With my background in postmodern literature, this work, at once a travelogue, journal, autobiographical fiction, and critical essay, made me feel at home in its hybrid and fragmentary form—apparently ideal for a post-structuralist reading—yet also transported me to a rather defamiliarizing territory, which challenged me to rethink many theoretical premises of postmodernism. To be sure, the nonlinear structure of the Danubian narrator's meditations problematizes monolithic identity, undermines teleology, interrogates the memory and places of official history, but its author does not give up searching for truth, even with the awareness that it can never be attained. Beyond delegitimizing and illusion-breaking stances, and despite the so-called postmodern waning of the affect, *Danube* allowed me to discover an author who not only writes critically but also *feels* critically about the complexities and contradictions of life.

I could consolidate these ideas after studying and teaching the entirety of Claudio Magris's works, with the additional privilege of team-teaching a course with Magris himself on his literary *oeuvre*—"From the Danube to the Sea: The Itinerary of an Italian and Mitteleuropean Writer." For my students and for myself, it was an occasion to fully appreciate how, even in postmodern or post-postmodern times, literature can not only exert the power to dismantle grand narratives and to decree the death of the subject but also facilitate its ethical rebirth.

Nostalgia, anxiety, nihilism, hope, suffering, and dreams of justice are emotions that Magris interrogates throughout his entire narrative and critical journey, in which disenchantment coexists with the need for resistance and accountability. In any scenario, life, as the title of one of Magris's books reminds us (*La vita non è innocente*), is not innocent. Each of us is implicated and responsible.

Magris is, indeed, "a local universalist" (Steiner in De Marco *Magris Argonauta* 53)—as the renowned French scholar George Steiner has aptly labeled him—rooted in the cultural space of his beloved native city of Trieste, and simultaneously open to the other, to the most authentic meaning of humanism as *nihil alienum*. What matters in literature, we read in Magris's essay collection *Utopia e disincanto*, are not the answers that the writer provides, no matter how exhaustive, but rather the questions he asks, which are always wider in scope (*Utopia* 28). The questions that Magris raises in his works are paramount and forceful, be they about the status of individual and collective identities, the mission of Europe, the responsibility of history, or the role of the humanities. But there is, in my view, a compelling overarching answer to all his inquiries. Even when facing the doubts generated by life's blend of authenticity and ambiguity, even when trying to untangle the knot of sense and nonsense in which we are caught, Magris has the courage to defend the search for values as a principle, able to direct thought and action, and to rely on the creativity of literature to help us in this pursuit, challenging a homogenizing cultural industry that reduces life to mere needs, efficiency, and utility.

My heartfelt thanks to Claudio Magris, for his encouraging feedback on different versions of this editorial project, and for having chosen my classroom at Georgetown University as one of his many temporary homes, keeping alive that domestic feeling ever since, with warmth and generosity.

I am very grateful to the two anonymous readers' supportive comments and thoughtful suggestions, as well as to Brigitte Shull and Ryan Jenkins at Palgrave Macmillan for their commitment to this book and their efficiency throughout the publication process.

I am deeply indebted to the precious research support I received from the National Endowment for the Humanities and from Brown

University's Howard Foundation, without which my fascinating journey into literary Europeanness could never have begun.

Special thanks to Sandra Parmegiani for having involved me in initiatives on Claudio Magris that allowed me to structure my project; to Elena Coda for having believed in this book and for her availability at crucial moments of its realization; and to Valeria Finucci for her advice at several difficult crossroads.

Unless otherwise stated, English translations (and all remaining shortcomings) are my own.

Introduction

Abstract: *For Magris the totalizing ambition of modernity is incompatible with our complex and disjointed present. However, he still believes in the ability of narratives to look for meaning, although never as a permanent acquisition. This condition of precariousness, which characterizes individual and collective identity, can be effectively visualized through a cluster of images and concepts related to actual or symbolic dwellings, which recur in Magris's works. With the aid of current theories by De Certeau, Tuan, and Bachelard on identity, location, and the abode as a physical and psychological site, the introduction illustrates Magris's challenge to both fanatic closure and rootlessness through the notion of "temporary homes," tracing its progressive expansion in Magris's spatial horizon, from the individual self as a private dwelling, to the communal homeland of nation and Europe, and, finally, to the dimension of writing.*

Keywords: Claudio Magris; home; Michel de Certeau; theories of space and place; topophilia; Yu-Fu Tuan

Pireddu, Nicoletta. *The Works of Claudio Magris: Temporary Homes, Mobile Identities, European Borders.* New York: Palgrave Macmillan, 2015. DOI: 10.1057/9781137488046.0003.

Claudio Magris's geography of domesticity

> one can never really possess a home, a space carved out of the universe's infinity, but only stop there, for a night or for a lifetime, with respect and gratitude.
> (Magris *Infinito* x)

Contemporary Italian scholar, writer, and translator Claudio Magris is one of the most prominent European intellectuals. In addition to volumes of literary criticism, from *Il mito absburgico nella letteratura austriaca moderna* (1963) [The Hapsburg Myth in Modern Austrian Literature] and *Lontano da dove* (1971) [Far from Where] to *Utopia e disincanto* (1999) [Utopia and disenchantment], *L'infinito viaggiare* (2005) [Infinite Traveling], and *Alfabeti* (2010) [Alphabets], down to the pamphlet *Segreti e no* (2014) [Secrets and Non Secrets], Magris is the author of numerous works of fiction, among them the much acclaimed travel narrative *Danubio* (1986) [*Danube* (1989)] and the impressionistic, autobiographical sketches collected in *Microcosmi* (1997) [*Microcosms* (1999)], the plays *Stadelmann* and *Le voci* [*Voices* (2007)], the theatrical monologue *Lei dunque capirà* (2006) [*You Will Therefore Understand* (2011)], and the novel *Alla cieca* (2005) [*Blindly* (2008; 2012)]. A renowned Germanist, he has translated into Italian works by Ibsen, Kleist, Schnitzler, Büchner, and Grillparzer, and is a columnist for the Italian newspaper *Corriere della Sera*, as well as a contributor to leading European journals. A member of the most important European academies, Magris has been awarded honorary degrees and numerous prestigious national and international prizes such as the French Prix du meilleur livre étranger in 1990, the Strega Prize in 1997, the biennial Würth Prize for European Literature in 2000, the Erasmus Prize and the Leipzig Book Prize for European Understanding in 2001, the Prince of Asturias Prize in 2004, the 2006 Austrian State Prize for European Literature, the Premio Viareggio Tobino in 2007, the Peace Prize of the German Book Trade in 2009, the 2012 Budapest Prize, the 2009 and 2014 Campiello Prize, and the 2014 Prize in Romance Languages by the Guadalajara International Book Fair. He has also been a favorite for the Nobel Prize in Literature.

Magris's European standing is not only due to his widespread international recognition but also to his multicultural personal world. Magris acknowledges an inner contradiction in his own intellectual background. His historico-philosophical perspective derives from German culture. His prose, especially its syntax, is rigorously Italian, whereas his literary and biographical venues—starting from his borderline native town Trieste—are, as he himself claims, anomalous and "other" with respect to Italian experiences (Magris and Ciccarelli 407). Although he feels at home in the Italian language, the world he portrays and attempts to organize through his mothertongue is composed of heterogeneous sensations and events that make him cross multiple frontiers. However, this discrepancy between the national dimension of his expressive tools and the boundless variety of stimuli to be processed does not deform reality in a destabilizing way. Rather, through the accumulation of different perspectives Magris attempts to get "al cuore delle cose" (408) [to the heart of things].

Claudio Magris's aesthetics could be defined with the words that Walter Benjamin adopted to describe the effects of Marcel Proust's blend of fiction, autobiography, and commentary in *La Recherche*: "everything transcends the norm" (Benjamin *Illuminations* 210), hence confirming that great works of literature are "special cases" (201) because they "found a genre or dissolve one" (201). Magris, too, is a special case. He combines the stylistic innovation of his hybrid forms with a rootedness in values that distinguishes him from the typical postmodern approach, with its challenge to the possibility of truth and meaning, the eclipse of reality and subjectivity, the breakdown of tradition not accompanied by the promise or intent to search for answers and to rebuild on the debris of the past. Just as the Danubian culture of which he writes "has with disillusioned clarity denounced the falsity of postmodernism, discarding it as stupid nonsense while accepting it as inevitable" (*Danube* 36), Magris himself admits that the epoch of grand narratives offering an unproblematic totality has come to an end, but the big questions of modernity for him are still open. Although he does not intend to resurrect the great modern season of the novel, whose totalizing ambition would be incompatible with our complex and disjointed epoch, he still believes in the ability of narratives to confront the disorder of the world and to look for meaning without the illusion to acquire it permanently. He thus distances himself from a simplistic and even material conception of foundation, yet he advocates the need to "continually found a totality" (*Quale totalità* 69) which, although temporary and always in progress, does not exempt us from "establishing meaningful connections" (70), despite awareness of the gap between our aspirations and our results.

Beyond the literary realm, grand narratives evoke, indeed, the "grands récits," the apparatus of discursive constructs (such as the emancipatory power of reason or the dialectics of Spirit) upon which, according to Jean-Francois Lyotard, modernity relied to legitimize knowledge. Instead of endorsing the postmodern "incredulity towards metanarratives" (Lyotard *Postmodernism* xxiv) contenting himself with "clouds of narrative language elements" (xxiv) or yielding to the power of the unpresentable, Magris maintains that history has not ended—as the title of his eponymous essay collection, *La storia non è finita*, asserts,[1]—although it can no longer be approached as a teleological expression of the Enlightenment project. Just as the classical literary tradition for Magris is far from static or dead, and can teach us to understand our times, the legacy of the past helps us account for the variety of life, which Magris neatly distinguishes from what he considers the anarchic fragmentation of postmodernism (*Utopia* 264). Although he questions the naively optimistic enlightenment that in the past underestimated the incongruities of reality and the complexities of irrationality, Magris reduces the power of reason to a feeble flame in the nocturnal darkness but still defends its necessity, recognizing that its precariousness makes it all the more precious as a means to confront our own limits. His approach is hence a "disenchanted enlightenment" (Magris and Parmegiani 151), the lucid awareness of the irrational foundation of reason but never ready to surrender to irrationality. Quite the contrary, disenchantment prompts Magris patiently and rationally to seek whatever portion of rationality can be attained, without clashing with feelings and imagination. Combined together, utopia and disenchantment hence suggest that the world can and has to be improved, although it can never happen once and for all, but, rather, along a trail full of defeats (Magris and Ciccarelli 410; Coda 376).

Despite Magris's remarkable visibility on the international literary scene, no book-length critical study of his works has been published so far in English. I decided to fill that gap with a comprehensive analysis of Magris's works from a new interpretive perspective able to help readers appreciate the continuity in his production and familiarize themselves with his less-known texts. "People speak of my hydrophilia, and there is (…), in everything I write, a great deal of water" (Magris, "Self That Writes" 21), Magris acknowledges in an autobiographical essay, "not solely the great waters of the sea and the river, but also that muddy water of the lagoon, and the pond" (21). Most critical studies on Claudio Magris, indeed, have explored the complex question of individual and collective identity in a selection of his essays and creative works through the motif of liquidity as Magris's main metaphor for a drifting self, embodied above all by the sea, especially in connection with the experience of travel and the ambivalence of the frontier. This is the case of the volume *Epica sull'acqua. L'opera letteraria di Claudio Magris* (1997) by Ernestina Pellegrini, to date the scholar who has mostly contributed to the visibility of Magris on the Italian literary scene, and, more recently, of the monographic study on *Danube* by Natalie Dupré, *Per un'epica del quotidiano. La frontiera in Danubio di Claudio Magris* (2009).

However, no systematic attention has been paid to a related cluster of images and concepts, revolving around actual or symbolic dwellings, which, in fact, in a dialectical tension with liquidity and travel, enrich Magris's poetics, interweaving home as the locus of autobiographical experiences and memories with the historical, political, and cultural underpinnings of the idea of homeland, ranging from the regional dimension to the national and transnational (especially European) ones. A Nietzschean image can effectively depict this idea of habitation grounded in fluidity: "I would not build a house for myself (...) But if I had to, then I should build it as some of the Romans did—right into the sea" (Nietzsche *Gay* 214). As a complement to Magris's well-known "hydrophilia" ("Self" 21), therefore, I propose to bring to the foreground what elsewhere I have already called Magris's "domestic topophilia" (Pireddu "On the Threshold" 333).[2] I adopt the term "topophilia" with the meaning that Yu-Fu Tuan assigns to it in his eponymous work defining the individual's "affective ties with the material environment" (*Topophilia* 93), and that in Gaston Bachelard's *The Poetics of Space* connotes love for a specific kind of space, precisely that of the house as a *"felicitous"* (*Poetics* xxxv), "eulogized" (xxxv) site, one that "has been lived in, not in its positivity, but with all the partiality of the imagination" (xxxvi). As Tuan observes in *Space and Place*, places are "organized world(s) of meaning" (*Space* 179) and "centers of felt value" (4). If "experience is compounded of feeling and thought" (9), the concept of home synthesizes the spectrum of modes through which the subject relates to reality, from perceptions and emotions to their symbolization.

Space and place for Tuan are interdependent ideas. The abstract and general notion of space becomes place when the subject's specific knowledge and personal experience ascribe value to it. In particular, although space is "that which allows movement" (6), it is a "pause in movement" (6) that transforms spatial location into place. "From the security and stability of place we are aware of the openness, freedom, and threat of space, and vice versa" (*Space* 6). Michel De Certeau in *The Practice of Everyday Life* seems to substantiate Tuan's dichotomy of space and place when he claims that a place is "an instantaneous configuration of positions" (*Practice* 117) implying "an indication of stability" (117), whereas space exists in connection with vectors of direction, velocities, and time variables, hence it is "composed of intersections of mobile elements" (117). Magris, however, blurs the difference between these two components of physical environment. It is through movement that both space and place generate meaning and values in his literary world, starting from the house as a foundational physical and psychological site.

My analysis of Magris's works starts from the premise that, as De Certeau maintains, the lack created by discourse "makes room for a void" (106) within habitable spaces, assimilating dwelling places to the presences of multiple absences. "Places are fragmentary and inward-turning histories, pasts that others are not allowed to read, accumulated times that can be unfolded but like stories held in reserve, remaining in an enigmatic state" (108). The "being-there" (109) in spatial practices acts "in *ways of moving into something different*" (109), that is, it amounts to being other and moving toward the other. Dislocation undoes the "readable surfaces" (110) of space and creates metaphorical and mobile ones. My examination of the connection between location and identity in Magris's poetics is predicated upon the idea that just as stories are "spatial trajectories" (115) that inscribe mobility into both space and place, the identity of the subject that inhabits those readable sites is equally temporary and precarious. The home that in Magris connects space, discourse, and identity is a place that undermines, rather than consolidate, what De Certeau defines as "the law of the proper" (117), the order through which place is supposed to distribute elements "in relationships of coexistence" (117) able to provide stability. Through the largely unnoticed motif that I term the "temporary home," Magris challenges ideological absolutism. In his creative and critical writings, notions like identity and homeland as provisional dwelling places, literature as relocation, and borders as thresholds authenticate a systematic reflection which, starting from the treatment of the self as a moving and mutable abode and from the home as the locus of an ongoing process of lodging and dislodgement, expands to the mobility of national and European identities.

As Magris avows, however contradictory it may appear, he considers himself "at the same time both nomad and sedentary" (Obrist and Magris). "Sedentary in the sense that I am very attached to things, to places, to the extent that even moving homes, from the first to the fourth floor would give me the impression of uprooting" (Obrist and Magris).

Although he defines himself "very stay-at-home and habitual" (Obrist and Magris), he overcomes the apparent incompatibility between repetitiveness and novelty by adding that he has "these habits everywhere, all over the world, with the same conservative pathos that is opposed to change" (Obrist and Magris). Far from surprising, this contradiction can be considered the foundation of his poetics. In his literary production Magris sees two kinds of writing at work, which he labels as "diurnal" and "nocturnal," drawing inspiration from Argentinian writer Ernesto Sábato's classification of his own fiction in those terms. As Magris has frequently explained, most recently in *L'infinito viaggiare* (xxiii–xxiv), *Alfabeti* (340–347) and *La vita non è innocente* (41–47), diurnal writing expresses the writer's conscious creation of himself and of the world, whereas nocturnal writing results from a more estranging process that gives voice to experiences and drives beyond the control of consciousness. As I hope to show, the temporary abode in his works represents the material or metaphorical site of a tug of war between those two conflicting realms—construction and disintegration, rootedness and distance, utopia and disenchantment—which recodifies individual and collective identities, histories, and memories as uncertain and provisional.

A writer whose life and work have been marked by multiple frontiers, as we will see throughout this book, Magris approaches this borderline spatial and existential condition with an attitude that is neither hopelessly tragic nor euphorically nihilistic. He delineates a paradoxical, ironic domestic space transcending both obsessive closure and nomadism *tout court*. Irony, he writes in *Utopia e disincanto*, dissolves rigid, imposed boundaries but builds human and flexible ones (*Utopia* 59). On the one hand, therefore, Magris's topos of the temporary home can be considered an example of what Tuan defines as "mythical space" (*Space* 86), namely, "the spatial component of a worldview" (86), "an intellectual construct" (99) and "also a response of feeling and imagination to fundamentally human needs" (99). At the same time, however, unlike Bachelard, Magris does not idealize homeliness. Quite the contrary, through the provisional nature of dwelling Magris problematizes self-sameness and self-consistency. Mobility renders the domestic space (be it the image of one's own self, the household, the nation, or a supranational entity like Europe) a form of personal, creative resistance to ideological strictures—above all, to the notion of identity as private ownership. Magris alerts us to the danger of "entrenching ourselves inside a cavernous interiority" (Magris and Parmegiani, "Colloquio" 154), and simultaneously rejects the opposite extreme—the nomadic subject that, for instance in Homi Bhabha or Rosi Braidotti, deconstructs identity through constant displacement, by relinquishing "all idea, desire, or nostalgia for fixity (...), without and against an essential unity" (Braidotti *Nomadic* 22). Magris's works map a geography of domesticity made of provisional places with concrete yet mobile borders where the subject lives in a symbiosis of rootedness and remoteness. Magris thus offers us a critical and poetic approach to being and belonging that still makes it possible to think "affectionately about home" (Said in *Nation* 116) as Edward Said claims, without falling into idolatry of the self or fanaticism of the homeland.

If every component of a place tells a story, what stories do we read in Magris's domestic geography? Through the filter of individual and collective memory, in autobiographical or fictional settings, narrators and characters interrogate the European literary, historical, and philosophical legacy, explore private and public sites as receptacles of contested meanings and values, and search for shareable principles. In each chapter of this book, the topos of the temporary home frames a particular aspect of the correlation of "who" and "where" in Magris's literary itinerary. Although I do not aim to be exhaustive, I examine most of Magris's production, including his most recent essay collections, which have not been translated into English or analyzed so far.[3] Instead of adhering to a chronological order, my chapters connect different texts following a logical thread that traces a progressive expansion in Magris's spatial horizon, from individual identity as private dwelling, to the communal spaces of nation and Europe, and, finally, to the dimension of writing itself.

In addition to offering a new perspective on the author's literary and critical trajectory, my interpretation wishes to highlight how, well beyond the domain of Italian literature, Magris's poetics and ethics of domestic spatiality can contribute to a wider cultural and theoretical dialogue on identity, location, and mobility engaging the humanities at large. Magris offers us a constructive, critical approach to the crucial question of the return to humanism that is moving literature and theory beyond the alleged death of the subject and of meaning.

Wandering in the rooms of his personal and intellectual life, Magris renders us dwellers of an encyclopedic boundless house, a world of global contradictions and local challenges and adventures that is certainly worth inhabiting.

Notes

1 This title poignantly reaffirms what Magris has declared throughout his career, namely, that "the current refusal of history is an aberrant phenomenon, equal to the worst and most myopic historicism" (Magris *Quale totalità* 60).
2 The initial results of my research on the topos of the temporary home in Claudio Magris's works were first presented in the panel "The Other Within: Claudio Magris's Europe and Beyond," which I organized for the conference "Europe in Its Own Eyes: Europe in the Eyes of the Other" at the University of Guelph on October 1–3, 2010, with Claudio Magris as the keynote speaker. The text of my address was published as "On the Threshold, Always Homeward Bound: Claudio Magris's European Journey," together with the other panelists' interventions, in a special issue of the *Journal of European Studies*, "Claudio Magris and European identity," edited by Sandra Parmegiani.
3 Ernestina Pellegrini's *Epica sull'acqua*—which provides detailed personal interpretations, close readings, and a contextual reconstruction of most of Magris's texts published until 1997—excludes the novel *Blindly* and all the numerous essay collections that Magris has written in the last 15 years, down to 2014. In her introductory essay to the first volume of Magris's collected works for *I Meridiani* ("Claudio Magris o dell'identità plurale"), Pellegrini, however, discusses many of those works, although not from the perspective I propose in this book. For her part, Licia Governatori in *Claudio Magris: l'opera saggistica e narrativa* offers a succinct descriptive and thematic introduction to Magris's works, less comprehensive and detailed than Pellegrini's book, and also excluding Magris's most recent literary contributions.

1
Households of the Self

Abstract: *Drawing from Bachelard and Heidegger's theories, this chapter examines Magris's conception of individual identity in connection with the motifs of home, language as dwelling place, and transience in the play* Stadelmann, *the narrative monologues* You Will Therefore Understand *and* Voices, *and the short novels* A Different Sea *and* Il Conde. *Magris's attachment to the human and aesthetic value of home does not render the latter a stable, private site of non-negotiable inclusions and exclusions. Just like identity is "making" and not "being," conquest and not permanent ownership, the supposed intimacy of the home is inseparable from the experience of the unknown. Through his characters' inability to accept precariousness and change, Magris shows that clinging to stability amounts to destroying life itself.*

Keywords: Gaston Bachelard; identity; language and being; *Lei dunque capirà* [*You Will Therefore Understand*]; Martin Heidegger and temporality; *Stadelmann*

Pireddu, Nicoletta. *The Works of Claudio Magris: Temporary Homes, Mobile Identities, European Borders.* New York: Palgrave Macmillan, 2015. DOI: 10.1057/9781137488046.0004.

1.1 *Stadelmann*: dwelling in the space of the "-ex"

> Our identity is partly made up of places, of the streets where we have lived and left part of ourselves. (Magris *Danube* 215)

According to Gaston Bachelard, in the life of an individual "the house thrusts aside contingencies, its councils of continuity are unceasing. Without it, man would be a dispersed being. It maintains him through the storms of the heavens and through those of life. It is body and soul" (Bachelard *Poetics* 6–7). Defined by many physical and symbolic dwelling places, from real houses and cities, to nations, languages, and cultures, Claudio Magris and his literary characters find images of intimacy in the house, precisely not simply as a result of mnemonic activity but also as a productive, creative force blending the real and the unreal, in a synergy of signification and symbolization. However, their attachment to the human value of the abode as a space to be loved and "defended against adverse forces" (xxxv) does not translate, as in Bachelard, into a stable, private site that determines non-negotiable inclusions and exclusions, setting up ideological or emotional differences with what is not home. As Magris explains in his essay "Personaggi dalla biografia imperfetta," when he decided to visit the real home of Enrico Mreule—the protagonist of his short novel *Un altro mare* (*A Different Sea*)—he was in search of those tiny objects and negligible private details from which the epiphany of a life can emerge. In fact, however, despite his immersion into that domestic world, Magris avows that the only biographies he can write of his characters are invented accounts, marked by incompleteness and fragmentariness (Magris "Personaggi" 618).

As in the mythical Homeric episode, coming back home "after an odyssey of many years" (*Poetics* 15) allows Bachelard to recover the same, faultless repertoire of memories and feelings. The dynamic relationship between journey and homecoming, lived experiences and their recollections, is equally crucial to Magris, for whom, however, the recovery of the domestic sphere that grants Ulysses respect and stability in Ithaca is inseparable from a "beyond," which not only is inscribed in the title of one of his essay collections, *Itaca e oltre*, but also informs his overall poetics.[1] The Homeric hero's journey is an itinerary that, from the unknown, leads back and ascribes truthfulness to the familiar precisely at the end, as a point of arrival, rather than a departure, and it is precisely the return home that consolidates the traveler's identity. However, our own Odyssey today is different. To the traditional, circular Ulyssean epos, which for Magris underlies the total, organic Romantic conception of the world that prompts Novalis to imagine the subject always homeward bound, Magris opposes the contemporary "rectilinear odyssey" (*Itaca* 47), a nomadism without Ithaca, prompted by a perpetual interrogation of the world. The modern Ulysses for Magris does not go back home confirmed in his own identity. He disperses and is estranged from himself, unable to recognize himself in the many faces he puts on and abandons in his centrifugal run, lost on the road toward infinity or nothingness (*Utopia* 59).

In addition to discovering and disclosing the precariousness of the world and of the individual self, travel for Magris "teaches us how to inhabit more freely, more poetically our own home" (*Infinito* x). The contemporary Ulysses is always a stranger and a guest, who feels simultaneously in the unknown and at home, and, by learning to be "Nobody" (x), he understands that it is never truly possible to own home and identity like properties but only humbly to station in them, be it for one night or for an entire life. Magris here not only evokes the *status viatoris* that connotes life as an earthly journey into finitude. By revising the staticity of the loyal Ulysses who yearns to go home and settle, he elaborates a notion of individual and collective identity in terms of temporary homes. Both the domestic hearth and the national birthplace for him are not rigid spaces to be mourned nostalgically through the lens of temporal or geographical distance but, rather, destinations shaped by the traveler's own path and transformations. As we read in his book-length essay on exile in Eastern European Jewish literature—*Lontano da dove*—it is precisely the failed prospect of a return that, however painful, can divest the individual of any "falsifying garment" (*Lontano* 83).

The 1988 play *Stadelmann* well demonstrates that, in Magris's poetics of domestic space, Tuan and Bachelard's notion of topophilia can hence function only with the awareness that recollections of comforting retreats cannot provide real relief for the present and do not offer, either, an undisturbed day-dream back into the allegedly felicitous past. The birthplace that we nostalgically look for in our bygone childhood can in fact be found only at the end of our homeward journey (*Infinito* xi), a journey which, however, does not conclude with circularity. The eponymous protagonist of the play is Goethe's former servant, Johann Carl Wilhelm Stadelmann, now old and forgotten, living in a poorhouse in Jena. Being among the very few surviving people who personally knew Goethe, Stadelmann is invited to Frankfurt for the inauguration of Goethe's monument. Back home, he gets drunk and hangs himself. Although it is Goethe's figure that hovers over *Stadelmann*, triggering the tension between the genius's greatness and the servant's marginality, this play is above all the stage of Stadelmann's own reminiscences, a patchy history of the self that marks the passing of time with a blend of nostalgia and resentment, dreams and disillusionment.

Although "we think we know ourselves in time" (Bachelard *Poetics* 8), Bachelard observes, all we know in fact is "a sequence of fixations in the spaces of the being's stability—a being who does not want to melt away, and who, even in the past, when he sets out in search of things past, wants time to 'suspend' its flight" (8). The function of space, for Bachelard, is precisely to compress time "in its countless alveoli" (8), which in *Stadelmann* are the spatial nooks of former dwellings that the protagonist retrieves through flashes of memory, looking in vain for self-confidence and self-consistency. Magris's play seems to authenticate the function of the house as an intimate site where recollections can stage what for Bachelard is "the theater of the past" (8). In fact, however, through those very house images that, as in a sort of *Bildungsroman*, Bachelard unproblematically considers promoters of psychological integration, Stadelmann's idealization of the past will fail.

After initially re-evoking a conversation between Goethe and his servant about the theory of colors, the play, indeed, shifts to a "squalid room, the parlor in the poorhouse at Jena" (*Stadelmann* 24) where an elderly and pensive Stadelmann further elaborates on those past memories. It is hence anything but Bachelard's "felicitious space" (*Poetics* xxxv) that hosts the protagonist's attempted self-recovery through recollections. Stadelmann clings to and settles in his personal household of the soul, the only abode that seems to allow him to define himself according to intimate personal experiences which, once materializing into his memory, disavow the reality of the present and cannot be shared with anybody else: "You need to have seen those colors, as I saw them myself—but who's going to see them now, without him who will show them to me and explain them" (*Stadelmann* 25). Therefore, the "proofs" or "illusions of stability" (*Poetics* 17) that the body of images constituted by the house allegedly offers according to Bachelard do not help Stadelmann enjoy a "eulogized" (xxxv) domesticity. The events staged in Stadelmann's recollections of his past and his personal interactions in the present continuously alter the nature and the psychological value of the domestic space, producing self-estrangement rather than a consistent "topography of our intimate being" (xxxvi). When the warden warns him to stay put—"Remember your place, Stadelmann" (*Stadelmann* 29)—in the Italian original, "State al vostro posto" (*Stadelmann* Garzanti 1988: 18), literally, "Stay in your place"—Stadelmann replies he would be glad to do so if only he knew what his place is. The inspector answers back by identifying Stadelmann's accommodation in the poorhouse as his sole abode and labels him as an "ex-servant" (*Stadelmann* 30). He thus implies that the value of Stadelmann's self is all gone, being attached uniquely to Stadelmann's former role as Goethe's attendant, and not applicable to his present status as a simple guest at the poorhouse. Yet, in his turn, Stadelmann reacts to this confining portrayal of his alleged current nothingness by specifying that "Everyone is an ex-, ex I don't know what, so many aren't even aware" (30).

Since, for Bachelard, "our soul is an abode" (*Poetics* xxxvii) and "by remembering 'houses' and 'rooms' we learn to 'abide within ourselves'" (xxxvii), the house images for him move in both directions: "they are in us as much as we are in them" (xxxvii). Yet, the exchanges between Magris's two characters generate conflicting interpretations of the connection of self and space. As the tension between "servant" and "ex-servant" in the previous repartee shows, Stadelmann thinks of himself as displaced in time and space, and considers his identity more than what his self is in the present moment, whereas the inspector limits Stadelmann by making his identity coincide only with those features that can and must be compatible with Stadelmann's current status. For the inspector, Stadelmann has lost a part of himself. For Stadelmann, however, every facet of the self survives, even though he realizes that everybody is something different from the past because we all share a condition of constant fluidity that affects the self as much as its spaces—its dwelling place in particular.

As though trying to recapture the virtues of Bachelard's shelter embodying the dreams and hopes of an identitarian continuity through time and space, Stadelmann defends his self-consistency by claiming, ironically, that in his life "it seems as if there was never anything new" (*Stadelmann* 38), and that precisely for that reason he never forgets anything. Yet, this conviction is at odds with pronouncements he recalls from Goethe, for whom there was no room for memory, as "there is no past of which to be nostalgic, everything is always eternally new" (38). For his part, the barber who prepares Stadelmann for his trip to Frankfurt for the inauguration of Goethe's monument seems to endorse permanence by remarking the difference between, on the one hand, the multifarious natural expressions of the human face—"a temporary face" (54)—and, on the other, an "ideal" (54) and "classic face" (54), an artifact "good for all occasions and uses" (54). Yet, significantly, the barber himself associates his ability to refashion the ephemeral instant into an eternal self-same to the art of laying out corpses for funerals, erasing the action of change by turning the human face into "a funeral mask" (54). Fluidity, change, temporality are exorcized at the price of life itself, an uncanny prefiguration of the play's ending, when Stadelmann takes his own life. Paradoxically, death crystallizes the human being in the very moment it decrees its end, its inexorable transience. Perversely, this will also be the moment when Stadelmann is offered a more reliable home and an annuity, both signs of material and emotional stability and continuity which he cannot expect to obtain in life. The surrounding "empty walls" (57) at which he ends up looking "as you look at a mirror" (57) are themselves a somber reminder of the "nothing" (57) that connects the abode and the self in Stadelmann's perception, both being expressions of privation, trespass, absence.

By mingling recollections and desires, truthful and imaginary details in their interaction with Stadelmann, the female figures in the play seem at first to substantiate what Bachelard presents as the cooperation of "the function of the real and the function of the unreal" (*Poetics* xxxv) in the human psyche. Bachelard's "poetics of the home" (xxxv) as "the space we love" (xxxv) assumes that the experience of the past, which memory grounds in positivity, has to be complemented with the alleged unreality of imagination as an equally productive force facing the future. However, Stadelmann's search for self-identity through the emotional reconstruction of a consistent domestic space associated with the women who crossed his path ultimately fails to recover the reassuring human value of intimate spaces and to defend them against temporal disaggregation and self-estrangement. It is the reverie of Steffi's past house—"it would be wonderful instead to go to your house, to your house from the old days" (*Stadelmann* 44)—that in Stadelmann's desires could offer him a protective, familiar shelter in lieu of the journey to Frankfurt that awaits him. What anguishes and destabilizes Stadelmann is precisely the geographical and emotional displacement that will compromise the stability and continuity he seeks.

As further compensation against the snares of the new and of the unknown, Stadelmann's fantasy conjures up another hallucinatory scenario of pseudo-domesticity, that of Madame Schnips's brothel, "a small way station for travelers who suffer from nostalgia" (33). This grotesque surrogate of the Bachelardian abode degrades the almost sacred coziness of domesticity to the experience of a vulgar and transitory intimacy. Significantly, in Stadelmann's visions the brothel ultimately overlaps with the poorhouse, another reversed double of the home as the custodian of emotions. Although the pimp's exclamation "The poorhouse is not a bordello and the bordello is not a poorhouse" (50) intends to separate the two places by accentuating their alleged deep differences, it shows with equal evidence how in fact the two places coincide in Stadelmann's mind, both representing misleading substitutes for profound, lasting emotions. Yearning precisely for a home as a domestic hearth, Stadelmann is left only with two pale copies of it.

Nevertheless, the play demonstrates that, whereas Stadelmann's emotional and mental universe coincides more and more precisely with the confining and ossified walls of the poorhouse, the outer world that Stadelmann had forgotten surprises him for its extension and heterogeneity, almost a reminder of the need to reside in one's own self as in a temporary home, the locus of identitarian fluidity. This idea emerges more consistently toward the end of the play, precisely when exposure to external memories creates a breach in the walls of Stadelmann's existential enclave. On the one hand, recalling his relationship with Goethe, Stadelmann seems to assert his identitarian autonomy and cogency, for instance when he claims he would not simply copy but actually write Goethe's journal. On the other hand, he also recognizes that "there is always something, you can do everything but get on with living" (66), falling back into a desire for permanence as a prerequisite for the consistency of the self, although in fact the self is inevitably undermined by elements that modify its nature. This is what Stadelmann himself conveys when he observes that "A true German looks to Europe and to the world" (70) borrowing Goethe's thoughts in the midst of a conversation with German interlocutors who support nationalistic closure. Although the Germans fanatically extol their homeland, Stadelmann upholds the wider value of humanity, hence endorsing once again his master's mental openness according to which "Germans will never be a people" (55).

Goethe, however, also reminds Stadelmann that this penchant for cultural pluralism is incompatible with self-consistency. When

Stadelmann hears the knells of the grandfather clock inside the house and those sounds of domesticity make his master think about his childhood, Goethe replies that the past does not exist, hence disavowing the homely space here invoked as the materialization of an idealized former stability and intimacy. Just as one of the customers at the inn reminds Stadelmann that the world and people change, hence it is impossible to "keep pulling the load as before" (71), another character, the Professor, reiterates Goethe's tormented sensitivity for "the frailty of man" (83)—even more explicitly, in the Italian original, "la caducità" (*Stadelmann* Garzanti 1988: 65) [caducity]. Although Stadelmann seems to reject this perspective, the Burgomaster's words authenticate it further by imagining the Goethian Faust as the spokesperson of a universal, unfulfilled desire for permanence, as he yearns to arrest the flowing of time: "moment, stop, you are beautiful."[2] Significantly, right before his death, it is Stadelmann himself who seems to confirm transience and precariousness when he formulates the need to arrest that fleeting moment. Meditating on the countless times one has to get dressed and undressed in a day, and comparing them to the condition of the crow which does not even have to do so once, Stadelmann's words also evoke the considerations on flux and identity underlying Cratylus's alleged revision of Greek philosopher Heraclitus's claim that you cannot step into the same river twice: for Cratylus, you cannot do so even once. It is not even possible to conceive of a complete self subject to external mutability. The self does not exist as a self-contained and complete entity in time and space.

Ending his existence is the only solution that Stadelmann can devise to overcome the lacerating conflict between the artificial uniformity of masks and the single and mutable reality of the human face—which Magris presents in his volume of essays *Utopia e disincanto* as the tension between "stiffening" (*Utopia* 60) and "dissolution" (60) of the self. Significantly, however, Magris recodifies in positive terms the condition that leads to Stadelmann's tragedy. Uncertainty, indeterminacy, temporality are for Magris the intrinsic feature of the I and of identity in its various forms. As he observes in his essay "Identità, ovvero incertezza," identity "seems to exist in the very doubt about itself" ("Identità" 519) and "should always be declined in the plural" (522) because the "I" itself is a multitude, a fluctuating entity. Identity is "process, creation, becoming" (522)—making and not being, conquest and not possession. Therefore, for Magris literature and writing are valuable precisely as acts of *poiesis*, constructions rather than mere representations that passively reflect a preexisting reality. Likewise, as he claims in *L'infinito viaggiare*, the home—the center of our lives, where we put our entire self at stake—is not an idyll (*Infinito* xix). Far from reassuring, it is the riskiest adventure, which can expose us to mistakes, conflicts, abuses, failures. Even more radically, home for Magris cannot even be attained or owned precisely because its supposed intimacy is inseparable from the experience of the unknown, along a precarious trail in which disintegration alternates with glimpses of a recognizable reality (x). If love of domesticity cannot but coexist with nomadic escape, in *Utopia e disincanto* Magris explicitly states that the self can only be hosted in a "casa provvisoria" [temporary home] (*Utopia* 61). The process of becoming that Magris conceives is not an abrupt rupture but, rather, the smoother mobility of a son who leaves his parents' home while coming back to it in his thoughts and feelings. What is lost is also renewed, in a ceaseless depaysement and return (69).

Magris, in other words, proposes an "ironic" (*Utopia* 60; "Personaggi" 620) attitude toward identity taken as an individual but dynamic unit, which he also adopts in the conception of his own fictional characters. As he further explains, once the harmony between the individual and his social totality is replaced by laceration and reciprocal incomprehension, as in the modern age, even the individual's relationship with his/her own self is marked by a fracture. Therefore, in order for an individual story to be authentic, it cannot but be disconnected, fragmentary, and imperfect ("Personaggi" 619). For their part, in contrast with what Magris's essays declare, Stadelmann and most of Magris's other characters are unable to accept their imperfect biographies, only made of splinters in the absence of the reassuring, albeit illusory, order of that household of the self which Stadelmann still yearns for.

1.2 At the self's door: *You Will Therefore Understand* and *Voices*

An equally poignant instance of this dialogical relationship between the character and the narrator's critical voices is the theatrical monologue *Lei dunque capirà* (2006) [*You Will Therefore Understand*],[3] which elaborates on places, questions, and relationships that *Stadelmann* had depicted, underscoring the existential but also metaphysical implications of the topos of the home as the meeting point of ephemerality and permanence, transience and eternity.

A woman living in a rest home addresses its elusive director—also a probable God-figure—explaining her decision not to leave her premises to return to life outside, against her desire and even though her companion came to fetch her. Initially presented simply as a nursing home where the female protagonist is waiting for her companion's visit, the "Home" (*You* 7) soon reveals a deeper significance, that of afterlife. Its capitalized initial, together with the solemnity and mystery that distinguish it from ordinary abodes, initially qualifies the assisted-living facility as a material and symbolic site outside and beyond the individual's earthly existence. Commenting on *You Will Therefore Understand*, Magris explains that a crucial element in the composition of this work was, precisely, "the threshold experience" ("Self" 28) which for him marked the difference between life inside and outside the nursing home. Yet, as the female protagonist's retrospective narrative progresses, the alleged differences between the two worlds are erased, just as in Bachelard's psychological spatiality "inside and outside, as experienced by the imagination, can no longer be taken in their simple reciprocity" (Bachelard *Poetics* 216). Rather, Bachelard claims, their dialectics "multiply with countless diversified nuances" (216). Although the woman mercifully lets her man in the illusion that the end of human life is also the end of transience, she does not spare us the revelation of a different truth by gradually dismantling that hope.

In her address to the invisible Director of the Home, the woman remembers the painstaking and complex rules with which she had to comply to leave the facility. We can hence surmise that there is no way back after relocating to the Home, and its feeble light also confirms the fixity and uniformity to which individuals—and the woman's companion in particular—aspire, hoping to stop change:

> it makes me feel like I'm at the bottom of the sea, where everything is fixed, motionless, even time (…); perhaps it was only down there, in the fixity of those instants long as centuries, that we were happy. But then even in here, down here, in this semi-darkness. (*You* 12)

Yet she also reveals to us that, contrary to usual claims, there is no big distinction between the Home and the external world, and that it is not even easy to realize when one is on either side. Enormous and unlimited but not endless, the Home apparently does not respond to the idea of an immobile eternity, and hence seems to promise the woman the chance of a way out. Indeed, as she recalls, she would run after her companion, pushing her way among the crowd, along the meandering corridors and landings that trace a very long but not infinite path, and claims she is ready to face the external world and her original domestic environment perhaps precisely because she has already perceived the analogies between the two homes.

According to Bachelard, "if the house is a bit elaborate, if it has (…) nooks and corridors, our memories have refuges that are all the more clearly delineated" (*Poetics* 8). In *You Will Therefore Understand*, however, the convoluted structure of the Home does not provide any emotional or rational support, but, rather, materializes and contextualizes the past and present turmoil of the two unsettled characters, and the hostile opaqueness of that dwelling place. The woman's companion, an Orpheus-like writer, attempts in vain to recover his beloved Eurydice in the underworld. Unable to content himself with impressions and reflections, he would like to use his poetic work to open the iron doors of the Home and unveil its secrets, or, rather, what he mistakenly thinks is the truthful reality of that impenetrable abode. For the protagonist's companion, the gleaming convex scales of the doors reflect the mutable and deformed broken images of things like fleeting caricatures. But Orpheus's avowed inability to sing only the mirages of those mirrors, and his intention to express with his verbal art that which for him holds the world together or disintegrates it persuades Eurydice to thwart her own rescue. Without her gesture, her Orpheus would have had the most painful revelation, precisely that of the lack of difference between appearance and reality, existential fluidity and identitarian fixity, "Home" and "home" as the self's dwelling place. Therefore, whereas the poet wants to tear Maia's veil of illusions and deformations and get to how things, hearts and the world really are, Eurydice prefers to sacrifice herself rather than allow her Orpheus to realize that transience and permanence are inseparable on both sides of the border marked by the "bronze doors that conceal destiny" (22). This condition of ephemerality and uncertainty that hinders all efforts to penetrate the secret of the origin and of the end, and prevents the woman from disclosing this tragic truth, brings together the two spatial and temporal scenarios—the two homes, the before and the after—in one single "immense labyrinth" (23), turning the nurturing and reassuring space of Bachelard's dwelling into the site of loss and estrangement *par excellence*.

Heartbroken by the loss of his Eurydice but unaware of the deep reason for her gesture, Magris's Orpheus returns to the world of impermanence still believing in a possible totality and stability enclosed within the walls of the Home, and allegedly finding an illusory serenity and sheltered happiness in a home with a small "h," "our house" (25), now asleep in the comforting habitual site of their past life together, hence also a surrogate for the communion that he could have reestablished with his woman if they had been reunited. Significantly, however, although this palliative domesticity seems soothing to him, we know through the woman's reflections—which convey the narrator's critical consciousness—that Orpheus is forced, against his will, to lay down his lyre before being able to reveal what nobody knows.

The considerations emerging from *You Will Therefore Understand* on home, death, and the impossibility of communication that confines each individual to the space of a personal enclave enrich the topos of the temporary home with Heideggerian elements, of which Magris's theatrical monologue may be said to offer a critical revision. The inexorable separation between Eurydice and Orpheus seems to decree the "non-relational, certain and as such indefinite" (Heidegger *Being* 303) nature of death, which, according to Heidegger, by breaking down the possibility of representation, consolidates the analogy between "mineness and existence" (284). In other words, by claiming that "death is in every case mine" (284), Heidegger emphasizes the singularity of the individual, who cannot share the experience of his/her own end (and ultimate wholeness, for Heidegger) with anybody else. With its final (although intentional) breakdown of communication, the epilogue of *You Will Therefore Understand* seems to confirm that "No one can take the Other's dying away from him" (*Being* 284). In Heidegger, however, this condition of singularity is not limited to the individual's final moment. If "[l]anguage is the house of being" ("Letter" 239) as Heidegger claims in his "Letter on Humanism," this human life that inhabits language is protected by, but simultaneously enclosed within this edifice, which, as it defines human essence, also creates a fracture, a separation from the world and from other individuals, each of them ultimately alone in their own, singular, monadic, house of being.

Although Magris takes issue with the Heideggerian notion of singularity, be it applied to the status of the individual or of collectivity,[4] *You Will Therefore Understand* seems to endorse Heidegger's difference between inhabiting and dwelling, which corresponds to a shift from linguistic praxis to *poiesis*. Unlike an inhabitant's simple physical, non-creative occupation of a space, in the home of language "human beings *dwell*"

("Letter" 239. Emphasis added), that is, are productive performers and agents of communication and exchange. For Heidegger, the "guardians of this home" (239) are poets, those "who think and those who create with words" (239). Just as a home is more than a simple residence precisely because of its emotional and psychological investment that transcends mere physical comfort, building can reconcile the individual with home by promoting a sense of belonging and of hope thanks to poetry. It is poetry as a productive expression that allows the individual to leave the singular house of being and open up to the plurality of beings through what Heidegger defines as potentiality, that is, the threshold between assertion and annihilation, vulnerability and enrichment.[5] The Orpheus of *You Will Therefore Understand* fails because, even more than Stadelmann, he expects to exit his house to find reassuring permanence in the Home rather than losing singularity and security in the very act of abandoning one's home and exposing one's own "unprotected being into the Open" (Heidegger "What Are Poets For?" 140)—as poets do according to Heidegger. Trying to protect his companion from truth, then, Magris's Eurydice makes him withdraw within the domestic walls of singularity, in the Heideggerian enclosed "precinct of language" (132).

Significantly, Magris's problematization of language as the house of being already appeared in the more obsessive setting of his 1999 play *Le voci* (*Voices*), where the home that hosts identity is, in particular, vocal performance, yet in this case deriving from the alienating artificiality of technology rather than from the intimacy of creative production. It is the monologue of an unnamed male individual who falls in love with female voices recorded in answering machines, calls them, and speaks with them, avoiding interaction with the real women. The plurality of recorded voices represents a static variety, a sum of fixed singularities not exposed to the risk—the poetic risk in the Heideggerian sense—of openness and potentiality. Voices remain contained each in its own respective enclave constituted by the recorded message. The male protagonist's calls to random homes in search of female recorded messages seem to prioritize momentary performances over permanence as he claims that "even with voices you must respect the timing and situation" (*Voices* 117). Soon, however, he begins to complain about changes in the recordings: "But who knows why, after all, she redid the recording, what must have come over her, like that, all of a sudden, to change the words" (118). The unexpected modification of the message text alters the reality he would have expected to find at each new call to that number. Fluidity and mutability hence thwart his attempt to fix a fleeting experience within the stability and consistency of the domestic walls.

Just as "a real word is only the one we write on paper, calm, alone in our own room" (*Voices* 119), only the homely, cozy, private environment seems to nurture a "real, understanding, necessary voice" (119), that is, for him, "the recorded one" (119). The answering machine can allegedly fix and hence authenticate once and for all what for Roland Barthes would be the individual "grain" articulated in the "very precise space of the encounter between a language and a voice" (Barthes "Grain" 181). Therefore, for instance, the real Laura for Magris's character is her voice "flowing like a wave, saying she wasn't home and inviting you to leave a message" (*Voices* 121). The recorded words are "her immortal soul, safe from the miseries of hoarseness" (122) and of all other accidental alterations, whereas the flesh and blood woman, whom he sees in the street with a colleague, is nothing more than "the simulacrum" (122) of herself. As he further explains: "It's the voices that count. Indeed, they are the only ones that exist" (122), almost as the "pure indication" (Agamben *Language* 32), "pure meaning to mean" (32) and "pure universal transcendence" (32) in Giorgio Agamben's conceptualization of language and voice in relation to the essence of subjectivity. In the protagonist's perspective, therefore, materiality and physicality are evanescent. Bodies seem to make much noise and occupy much space but in fact "they are just shadows, that disappear when the sun goes down" (*Voices* 122), whereas permanence is to be found in an allegedly immaterial manifestation like voice, what in Agamben is the space of "pure being" (*Language* 34). Indeed, as the protagonist soon specifies, the phenomenal reality of voices is everywhere around us. "[R]eal, corporal" (*Voices* 123) voices constantly come to us, but he warns us against their inauthenticity.

The protagonist feels supported by the alleged intimacy of the domestic environment where messages are generated and played, and by the love he draws from the female voices to which he listens. Soon, however, the coziness of the home and of language as repositories of the human, emotional experience he is seeking are violated by the synthetic messages produced by the anonymous and artificial "iron throat" (*Voices* 137) of an answering service. From the reassuring repetition with a difference that would gratify him in the framework of his illusory stability, he is now suddenly thrown into the alienating world of mechanical reproduction, obliged to interact with an "inhuman non-voice, that steel thing that talks (...) that out-of-tune, strident metal"

(139). The dehumanizing effects of *technē*, be it the answering machine or its more diabolical surrogate, render the domestic environment of *Voices* a simple residence to be physically inhabited, rather than a dwelling in Heideggerian terms ("Building" 145–161), one able to provide creative stimuli. Within the suffocating walls of the homes that his imagination reaches at each contact with a recorded voice, the protagonist refuses the hazard of potentiality, the open and transitory nature of the real world. He will rather try to compose other numbers to find some new real voice, searching that virtual domestic space for authentic and consistent selves, getting on with his impossible attempt to make the vocal space of pure being coincide with pure otherness, challenging change without ever giving up.

1.3   Hosting life in the moment: *A Different Sea* and *Il Conde*

The *impasse* of the protagonist of *Voices* emerges not only from the Quixotic nature of his quest for stability and permanence, but also from the ironic tone with which the narrative voice relates it, conveying the author's critical distance from his character's aspirations. In two earlier short fictions, *Un altro mare* [*A Different Sea*] and *Il Conde* [The Count], Magris offers us other instances of what I would call reversed micro-*Bildungsromane*, minimal, essential life itineraries of characters who, like the protagonist of *Voices*, are doomed to defeat instead of evolving along the lines of self-development because they cannot reconcile precariousness with their yearning for permanence.

A Different Sea, published in 1991, is a brief novelistic interior biography of the young Italian scholar Enrico Mreule, a close friend of philosopher Carlo Michelstaedter's, who in 1909 leaves Italy for Patagonia, withdrawing into solitude and anonymity in an impossible search for authentic life that ends with a progressive mental and physical deterioration after his return, 13 years later, to his confining Friulian turf. The expectations that Enrico formulates about his journey right before departure announce his attempt to reconcile displacement and staticity: "This voyage will be no escape, his departure no form of death. It will on the contrary come to represent life, existence, and an unshakeable stand" (*Different* 10). Recollecting Carlo's theories, Enrico, through the narrator's third-person, defines "persuasion" (56) as "the full ownership, both in and for the present, of one's self and one's life. It is the capacity to live each moment fully, without sacrificing it to what it is still to come, to something one hopes is just around the corner, thus destroying life by wishing away the present" (56). For its part, "rhetoric" (56), which stands for the social organization of knowledge and action, is like "an enormous barrier" (56) that individuals build to conceal the consciousness of their own vacuum.

Indeed, in *La persuasione e la rettorica* Michelstaedter had tackled the absence of foundations in modern life, which for him precipitates incessantly under its own weight. This downward movement prevents total possession of one's life. Yet immediate, total self-possession without any lack or expectations from the future would amount to the end of life itself (*Persuasione* 24–25). Magris defines Michelstaedter's work as a great diagnosis of the inability to live the moment in its transience, without absorbing it into a program or project ("Personaggi" 630). With his dislocation to Patagonia Enrico engages with what Carlo's philosophy conceives as an empty life. He experiments with non-being, attempting to live in an eternal present without the interference of rhetoric, that is, culture, knowledge, civilization. Convinced that existence is consumed by desire, he adopts the austere and solitary life of the gaucho as a model. If for Carlo the urban space is a community that assembles the weak, the open spaces of Argentinian pampas constitute a "blankness" which, as Ann Kaminsky observes, "offers no distraction to the self in-making" (Kaminsky *Argentina* 53), the "perfect space of emptiness" affording Enrico "a place to grow strong" (53).

Starting from the title, the plot seems to revolve around the tension between two bodies of water, the Adriatic sea of Enrico's birthplace and the ocean leading to Enrico's South American temporary adoptive country. Yet, for Enrico the sea is too much, because it evokes a promise of happiness and a search for meaning that he cannot accomplish. Enrico's struggle between the infinite and the limit has temporal and spatial implications, as it translates into a tug of war between the fleeting present and the absolute, and simultaneously between borderless and enclosed spaces. In the most relevant turning points of the story, this conflict is articulated through dwellings, which, in contrast with the openness of ground or water expanses, frame the character's adventures and feelings, exposing his inner lacerations. The "dingy classrooms" (*Different* 1) of Enrico's high school years already conveyed the disturbing sense of something missing and increased the desire for natural landscapes.

The ship now taking Enrico to South America on an ocean that to him is "monotonous and without limit" (2) offers him a refuge in staticity, as he is never tired of "the unchanging things" (2). Onboard the ship, "[h]e himself is not actually moving. Even those few steps from his cabin to the deck or to the dining room seem out of place in the grand stillness of the sea" (6). From the porthole, the window of his temporary home on the ocean, Enrico sees "the dark and angry water. Water and spray seem identical, their antiphony incomprehensible" (16). Just as the bunk in his cabin harbors his thoughts and reminiscences, the coffeehouse where he spends his first hours of the ship's call in Almeria provides order and concentration away from the surrounding turbulence.

Both enclosed spaces are substitutes for the attic that hosted all his enlightening intellectual exchanges with Carlo, an ambivalent site at once the cradle of Carlo's philosophical masterpiece and the hiding place of the gun with which Carlo would ultimately take his own life. Enrico will be directed by "the trigonometry of that attic room" (4), attempting to measure and channel thoughts and actions according to that domestic reference point. Just as Carlo "often stayed inside the house by the beach" (12), savoring that "peace of ceasing from fretful action" (12) also evoked by the etymology of his female friend's name Argia, in Enrico's Argentinian hut time flows according to a "more elastic, indeterminate" (38) measure, in synergy with nature's rhythms and changes. The freedom of "No-need" (42) according to Carlo "appears in both circles: in that of happiness, founded on being and values, which needs nothing—because it exists; and in that of death, which likewise needs nothing—because it does not exist" (42). But Enrico, settled in "the bit of ground which (...) belongs as much to the open prairie as to the enclosed space of his cabin" (42) realizes that "[b]oundaries on all sides both separate and unite so many different things" (42). He himself feels he "is at a boundary" (42) yet he does not know on which side he is: "Is he on the south-eastern frontier of happiness, or on death's north-western border?" (42). The narrative itself bridges the actual spatial and temporal gaps between the two characters by welding them together through the uncanny synchronicity of their respective actions, although geographically apart: Enrico shooting at a wild duck and Carlo at himself.

Additional transient spaces of domesticity define his return to Italy. At the "Pensione Predonzani" (*Different* 62) where he retreats in the secluded village of Salvore at the tip of Istria, the temporary well-being that Enrico seems to draw from this refuge is, however, perturbed by instability, by the tension between attachment to his own land and the "longing to escape" (63) that the other guests from the Danubian region convey, aggrandizing his personal struggle. In the silence and peace granted by the provisional comfort of his boat, Enrico has the illusion that the Schopenhauerian echoes of its name, "Maia," will also lead him more easily to "the pure present of things" (67). Yet the "milky blue bound by no shore" (67), toward which the boat's "white sail—the veil of *Maia*" (67) seems to take him, clashes in fact with a frightful painful counterpart, that of the harsh confines of the prison where later on Enrico will be locked after being mistakenly arrested by Yugoslavian dictator Tito during the invasion of Friuli. In the closed space of the prison cell, death impends not as the end of physicality, in line with Schopenhauer's asceticism, but, rather, as the culmination of the physical experience of suffering and pain inscribed in the body:

> Sweat's fetid stench pervades the airless room—not the sweat of a summer's day or of honest work, but the acid sweat of fear. Not to fear death and not to fear its companion, the fear of death—but the life of persuasion is difficult in practice. It is not easy to tolerate the stench, the interrogations, the beatings; it is hard not to hope at every moment that they will cease, open the door, and let one leave. (88)

The door does, indeed, ultimately open. Enrico is released, and, convinced that "freedom exists in nothingness" (28), he resumes his efforts to "dim, to dull the perceptible, as did Buddha, and not to notice that mutability of things" (95). This impossible, uncompromising quest ends, together with his life, in the last two enclosed sites of his tormented existential travel, where his self shrinks together with his space—the hospital room and his own bedroom in his house at Salvore, which Magris will visit to capture the way in which his character traversed existence ("Personaggi" 631). The author will open that "large studded trunk by the window" (*Different* 103) where family members gathered Enrico's volumes and objects, the last surviving traces and the memory of this tragic figure who, attracted by the two extremes of the infinite and nothingness, fails to dwell in the middle ground, in the tension that temporality and movement generate between the two. The present for Enrico never becomes absolute time but remains only a frigid, inert transit station (Pellegrini *Epica* 129).

The temporary homes in *A Different Sea* hence provide the scenario in which Magris stages the drama of Enrico's inability to live in the provisional stability of the present, which in fact is the premise of Magris's mobile identities. Unlike Enrico, Magris believes that we can only (and we have to) experience the absolute through imperfection, catching a glimpse of it through mediations, as we live in the time of history and not in a Platonic sky (Magris "Mio romanzo" 32). Not accidentally, the sea that brings at least temporary joy to Enrico and Carlo is not the virtually borderless ocean, "the sea of nothingness, shapeless and bitter" (*Different* 14) where nothing happens. Rather, it is the enclosed Adriatic sea, which synthesizes the liminal condition of "the boundary" (42), that of a happy fluidity and its deadly proximity to the solidity of the earth, an emotional and geographic threshold where freedom and containment coexist. Significantly, this dualism of sea and gulf is what renders the Adriatic a small-scale Mediterranean according to Predrag Matvejević (*Mediterraneo* 56–57), as it displays the variety and movement that characterizes the *mare nostrum*, with its ambivalence between openness and closure, at once crossroads and locus of conflicting coexistence.

Along this line, in Magris's short monologue *Il Conde* (1993) [The Count]—where an anonymous fisherman of cadavers recounts the story of his life at the service of the "Conde," the overbearing count and master of the Portuguese river Douro—the "mare-fiume" (*Conde* 24) [sea-river] can be considered the temporary home of the boatman's existence, insofar as it connotes the trespass of his many and fleeting identities, just as it determines the lot of the drowned:

> I the crew, sailor and harpooner and steward and deep-sea diver, nobody and many, it seemed to me I could drown once and twice, and many other "I"s of mine would have been left, many lives I have lost on the river, my father lost one, his own, but I have never had mine and I don't even know what I have lost or not lost. (24–25)

This experience of transience hence also depicts identity as expropriation rather than as permanent possession of reality because, as the boatman states, "as soon as one thing has gone by we do not know any more to whom it belongs and who got it" (10). On the one hand, the narrator claims that "all things are the same, one is worth another, and even happiness and unhappiness are the same" (25). On the other hand, however, the water that infiltrates the wood of the boat "dilating the holes more and more" (42) alludes to a material and symbolic alteration that consumes physical permanence as much as the individual's consistency, to the detriment of uniformity and sameness:

> Every day something pours away from me and makes me lighter, I feel like that little bit of mesh between two holes, and every now and then a piece comes off, two or three holes become a bigger one until there is only one hole, that is, not even that. (42)

Significantly, the entire monologue is set inside the fisherman's home, which constitutes not simply a material shelter defending the protagonist from the violent rain as he rekindles his memories but also a symbolic place guaranteeing a temporary detachment from the merciless power of water, a peaceful break from the oppressing presence of death as material and emotional obliteration. Here we are confronted with the relational, differential value that Bachelard ascribes to house and universe when, in an analysis of a poem by Baudelaire, he highlights the "protective center" (Bachelard *Poetics* 39) of the home against the backdrop of a hostile external environment. We "feel warm *because* it is cold out-of-doors" (39). In other words, "the house's value as a place to live in" (40) grows as the threat of the outside world diminishes, and the intimacy of inhabiting is thus experienced "with increased intensity" (41).

This interdependence of home and universe can offer an effective interpretive framework to a pivotal moment in *Il Conde*, which further emphasizes the dialectic of fixity and mobility at the foundation of Magris's poetics. After the two characters find a figurehead in the river, the protagonist saves it from the Count's axe and takes it home. This wooden female, a symbol of the liquidity of maritime life yet now sheltered in the fisherman's dwelling and able, in its turn, to convey intimacy, can be seen as a synthesis of temporary stability, being the trait d'union between the sea with its eroding, annihilating effect and the abode as the womb-like repository of female warmth and protection. Earlier in his meditations, the fisherman had admitted that only a woman can infuse "that good and great certainty (...) that happiness and mercy and smile" (*Conde* 11–12) able to help him withstand the snares of destiny, thanks to those intimate moments when he could put his head on her lap or feel her leg on his own, in a peaceful domestic setting. The female care and affection embody home for him, and it is precisely this maternal domesticity that the boatman seems to revive by bringing the wooden surrogate woman to his dwelling, next to the fire, the literal hearth and the symbolic heart of his household, as though the figurehead could transfer to the abode the protection she is believed to bestow upon the ship.

But, in addition to evoking the nurturing security of home and womb, the figurehead is also the everchanging sea, and the constant metamorphosis of her visage in the flickering glare of the flame summons plurality through the features of the boatman's various women—Nina, Maria, Giba—which overlap in his recollections, scroll, and pass by. And just as the lips, the hair, the breasts of these female evocations are different and mutable yet always the same, the boatman would like to go back to sea attaching the figurehead to his boat, but then concludes that a river or another are the same because water is the same everywhere, and "all's well that ends well or even just ends" (51). Therefore, although less assertively than Stadelmann or Enrico Mreule, with this final claim endorsing definitive closure also the fisherman of *Il Conde* formulates a desire to terminate multiplicity and the continuous flux of life, while recognizing his powerlessness against the inexorable action of time. Instead of attaching the figurehead to his boat and brave the water again, he and his female simulacrum close the monologue by reinforcing their attachment to domestic snugness.

In the face of mutability and precariousness, Magris's fictional characters cling to what in Bachelard is the stability offered by the "protective value" (Bachelard *Poetics* xxxv) of the house. Through his characters' failure, however, Magris does not endorse fear of loss or the pessimism of renunciation. Rather, he reinstates plural, trespassing identities as the intrinsic feature of the self, showing that to resist mobility, fluidity, and change amounts to absorbing and destroying life itself. "Defence is good, but if one only defends oneself in the face of life, one doesn't live, one dies, like somebody who fearing to be poisoned refuses to eat" (Magris "Self" 19).

Notes

1. For a discussion of the myth of Ulysses in Magris's treatment of European identity, see my "European Ulyssiads."
2. Translation mine. The Italian phrase—"attimo, fermati, sei bello!" (*Stadelmann* Garzanti 70) appears in the English translation of *Stadelmann* as "a moment, wait, you are beautiful!" which has either missed the sense of the original or at least rendered it in an ambiguous way.
3. *You Will Therefore Understand* has been staged in many Italian theaters among which Il Piccolo in Milan. An abridged version in Slovenian was

also produced at the Teatro Stabile Sloveno in Trieste on April 12, 2012, directed by Igor Pison. *You Will Therefore Understand* has inspired Giorgio Pressburger's film *Dietro il buio* (2011).
4 See Chapter 3 for additional comments on Magris's reflections about Heidegger, singularity, and *Heimat* in *Danube*.
5 For a discussion of Heideggerian potentiality in these terms see Bartoloni *Cultures* 125.

2
Homely Memories, Promised Homelands

Abstract: *In Magris's works, both the private site of the self and the geo-political landscape are surrounded by provisional domestic boundaries. The frontier identity epitomized by Magris's hometown Trieste connects the two realms. This borderline, multicultural city shows its positive and negative sides, being at once a heterogeneous space allowing its dwellers to discover the intrinsic otherness of the self and an alienating site that constantly dislocates the self, as emerges from the play* La mostra. *The idea of home locatable only in the very search for it, either as an abode within ourselves or as a land that one never possesses but rather leaves or seeks, has been present in Magris's fiction since his earliest work,* Inferences from a Sabre, *where homeland is a mobile space constantly displaced between the memory and the promise of an illusory lodging.*

Keywords: frontier identity and the other; *Illazioni su una sciabola* [*Inferences From a Sabre*]; *La mostra*; nation; Trieste; Vito Timmel

Pireddu, Nicoletta. *The Works of Claudio Magris: Temporary Homes, Mobile Identities, European Borders.* New York: Palgrave Macmillan, 2015.
DOI: 10.1057/9781137488046.0005.

2.1 A nomad and fugitive abode: Trieste and its narratives

> Culture means (...) to realize that the love for the landscape we see from our window is alive only if it opens up to a relation with the world. (Magris *Utopia* 67)

The transience of self and home which, as we have seen, subjects individual identity to expropriation rather than consolidate it as permanent possession can also help us appreciate the transition from private stories to public history in Magris's literary journey. In his fiction, the recurring reflections on a plural and mobile yet unitary identity symbolized by the temporary home transcend the personal and existential level, providing the framework for questions of national and supranational consciousness, collective memory and cultural belonging. Just as individual identity implies renewing our origins accepting to lose our childhood abode (*Utopia* 69), homeland cannot be held and owned as our own exclusive property. Love of home, be it a city, a region, or a nation, cannot be demonstrated, for Magris, through a barbaric celebration of turf and blood (69), but, rather, through the experience of loss. As identity for Magris is tantamount to uncertainty, and biographies are always imperfect, any site of collective belonging, be it home, the mythical regional community of *Heimat*, or a national or transnational homeland, has to be inevitably porous, open, unstable.

The flexibility and plurality embedded in the notion of precarious dwelling are the distinctive features of Magris's native town, the changing and multifaceted Trieste permeating his works. "As if by passing from a room to another in one's own house, it can happen that something that was familiar up until that moment will show itself strange or disquieting" ("Self" 2), Magris avows. This "identity of known/unknown" (2) has shaped his experience as a Triestine dweller in a period when the city, a crossroads of cultures, languages, ethnicities, and nationalities, was also physically cut in two by the frontier between the Italian and the Yugoslavian jurisdictions, experiencing at once the proximity to the threatening totalitarian regimes of Eastern Europe and the condition of a decentered town, neglected by Italian and Western European eyes. "I felt that, in order to grow up, I would have to cross that border, not simply with a passport but also spiritually, to make mine that world which was already mine" (2). Magris here effectively synthesizes the tension between ownership and dispossession at the roots of cultural belonging and connects it to the experience of the border, which, as he frequently acknowledges and as critics have further stressed, is central to his works.[1] "Many of my books are concerned, in different ways, with borders of all kinds—national, political, psychological, social, as well as borders within ourselves, between the different components of our Self" (3). I argue that, given the liminal condition it depicts, the border in Magris functions in particular as a threshold taken precisely as an expression of the domestic domain, that is, as the material limit that at a door marks the passage from one room to another, or from the inside to the outside of a house—as in the case of the rest-home in *You Will Therefore Understand*—and, more generally, from one condition to another—as *Danube* and *Microcosms* well demonstrate—separating but also connecting the two spaces or conditions despite their apparent differences. In *Utopia e disincanto*, indeed, Magris asserts that, provided we are conscious of their relativity, we should accept our own boundaries, as we accept those of our own homes (*Utopia* 61).

Significantly, to the interviewer of the architectural journal *Domus*, who, back in 1985, asked him whether he had an ideal, imaginary house in mind, Magris replied by describing an eclectic but organic dwelling able to synthesize and overlap, like a cubist city, all the places that he loved and that were pivotal to his development. Significantly, this heterogeneous assemblage is, for him, not a given, self-contained totality but, rather, an open universe, constantly in progress, accessible through the ugly church door of his childhood neighborhood, yet also representing "a kind of door to paradise" (Magris and Rinaldi 52) behind which there is a place where contradictions are absent or compatible. The emotional connection that Magris here makes between a provisional, unstable abode and the city becomes central to a more recent interview, where he transforms his previous references to his ideal house into a description of the city itself in his mental geography. He resorts once again to the image of the "cubist city" (Obrist and Magris) whose juxtaposed components are all the sites and landmarks connoting the most relevant episodes in his life. There are, above all, Trieste and the sea, together with Turin and its hills, but also many other sites that have hosted him in various parts of the world during his travels, like all the cafés which, in addition to the Triestine Caffè San Marco where he regularly writes, become temporary abodes in Paris, Freiburg, Munich, or Barcelona.[2]

Rather than acknowledge the home as the material and conceptual core of permanence, Magris's representation of Trieste lingers on the "sense of extreme precariousness" ("Self" 3) underlying the dialectics of bonding and mobility in his own approach to existence. The "feeling of being at the periphery of life and history" (2) in his borderline native town becomes a condition that, in contemporary life, applies equally well to "those who live at the world's centre, a centre which today no longer exists" (2). The heterogeneity of Trieste already represents a model for the contradictory nature of modernity in the critical monograph *Trieste. Un'identità di frontiera*, which Magris wrote with historian Angelo Ara. The opposite of synthesis and interaction, the city's "heterogeneous coexistence" (Magris and Ara, *Trieste* 113) is a bundle of dissimilar and incompatible constituents, yet it is only through dissociation that a reality emerges able to mirror the human condition and to reproduce the Babel of modernity. Recalling a famous claim by modernist Mitteleuropean writer Robert Musil, who defined himself as an Austro-Hungarian minus the Hungarian, that is, the result of a subtraction that differentiated him from pure, monolithic nationalities, Magris's hometown is an accumulation of disparate elements devoid of a central foundation, and not reconcilable in a unity of values. Hence, Triestine citizens find it hard to define themselves in positive terms. It is easier for them to proclaim what they are not, what differentiates them from any other reality (5). For this reason, Magris even assimilates the structure of Trieste to the composition of the Hapsburg empire itself: just as the attempt to solve the empire's intrinsic contradictions would have decreed its very end, Trieste, as a concentrate of empire, perishes with each univocal solution (7).

Although the creation of the freeport in 1719 attracted citizens of diverse origins to Trieste, the birth of the alleged multinational town for Magris is in fact a blend of reality and myth. Magris remarks that each dweller feels different not only from his/her neighbors, perceived as antagonistic opponents, but even from his/her alleged brothers. The only form of commonality that seemed to bring together those incongruent groups was the idea of a distant homeland, only identifiable with its fantastic projection (9). Not even the bureaucratic centralization attempted at the end of the eighteenth century by the Austrian emperor Joseph II could homogenize Trieste's multiple centrifugal drives. The pressure of Germanism, perceived as the imposed force of the state rather than a catalyst for national cohesion, has constantly clashed with the aggregating power of Italian language and culture upon migratory fluxes. To this profound laceration the additional assertion of Slovenian identity and culture should be added, which remains separate from the Italian reality. Therefore, Magris warns us against excessive simplifications and idealizations of Triestine cultural multinationalism, underlining that the latter is above all an elitist phenomenon, the exception rather than the rule. At the same time, he foregrounds the dramatic condition of Trieste, a city claimed by two peoples and torn between contrasting aspirations, yet nonetheless exerting its unifying force upon its components. "Triestinità" can hence be characterized as a condition of nonbelonging, which paradoxically constitutes the only possible condition of authentic belonging for country-less individuals.[3]

For Magris, the most emblematic dimension that exemplifies or even creates a symbolic homeland for Triestine identitarian homelessness is literature, which, starting from the experience of modernist writers like Scipio Slataper and Italo Svevo, can give expression to the poetic phantom of the writer's life. Literary identity thus becomes the Triestine subject's only true motherland, which otherwise could not be localizable in a definitive way. Taking literally Michel De Certeau's conceptualization of the space of the city as an "urban text" (*Practice* 93), Trieste for Magris *is* literature because it is through literature that the city gains a face, and, in its turn, literature acquires an existential value, promoting the Triestine citizens' search for truth because writing ascribes them not only an individual but also a group identity (*Trieste* 8). But if Trieste is, as Magris presents it also in *Itaca e oltre*, the place of writing (*Itaca* 281), this place is the epitome of instability and movement, features that its writers fully embody. Indeed, in a city historically dominated by the economic pursuits of an aggressive bourgeoisie—the very protagonist of modernity—where literary activity was not supported by any official cultural institution, the writer was obliged to be "un randagio ed un transfuga" (*Trieste* 35) [a homeless and a deserter]. His identity has hence been as precarious and mobile as the temporary sites where his writing could take shape. The locus of literature, indeed, is not represented by the literary circle but rather by the office (as in the case of Svevo's desk at the bank), or the backroom in Saba's bookstore, the café, or the tavern in Joyce (35).

In *Itaca e oltre* Magris avows that, for himself too, growing in Trieste meant and still means realizing to be living in a city made of paper, that is, covered by literature (*Itaca* 281). Emphasizing the rich literary tradition that his hometown has introjected and generated in its turn, Magris connects Trieste's indeterminable and misunderstood diversity to the locus of writing because it is in the realm of literature that the uncertainties and contradictions of identity can be exposed without attempting to reconcile them. Identity thus becomes a journey in search of itself, rather than an accomplished conquest. Certain truths, Magris claims in *Itaca e oltre*, cannot be described or declared, unlike theorems or ideologies. They can only be narrated, through stories with specific characters and events. The relationship between a writer and the places that condense the images of his own world is one of those truths that defy rational exposition, requiring, instead, the intervention of creativity (279). In the case of Trieste, in particular, this expressive difficulty translates an actual diversity with respect to other Italian towns. Its precarious yet unavoidable synthesis evokes a non-existing homeland, as no place can offer complete identification. Triestine time, too, is a non-time, a heterogeneous and disconnected mosaic, an always deferred promise (283). In this provisional state, the individual feels like a clandestine passenger of history, and it is precisely by being suspended at the margins of life that the need to write is born, because words, with their endless deferral of meaning, reproduce and substantiate the individual's experience of decenteredness, incompleteness, and continuous escape.

In *Itaca e oltre* Magris visualizes this spatio-temporal precariousness with a simile that highlights once again the centrality of the housing topos in Magris's imaginary. Trieste is like "una stanza" (282), a room that a writer traverses by reliving the totality of his existence in an atemporal instant as in a collage where everything is present and contiguous. If, as Magris writes in his narrative "Trieste," time in his hometown becomes space, this space is itself unstable, provisional, disorganized. It underscores the blend of domestic intimacy and extraneousness in an urban realm made of events stacked next to one another, as "in a warehouse of History" ("Trieste" *Atlante* 52), where objects and thoughts are intermingled without any order, in a heterogenous mix. At the opposite end of the intimate, affective, poetic space of the home, the image of the warehouse evokes an anonymous, prosaic building, accommodating merchandise instead of feelings. Connoting Trieste as a cold, soulless city, incapable of stirring emotions, the warehouse brings back to the foreground a fundamental aspect of its history and identity, namely, that of a mercantile town, gentrified through trading, which, as a protagonist on the European commercial scene, had even become a stop for the Orient Express on its way to the Balkans. Significantly, however, precisely for this mercantile essence, Trieste had also earned the label of a city without cultural traditions, as writer Scipio Slataper forcefully claimed in his famous essay on his hometown (Slataper *Scritti* 3–7). Like Dostoevsky's Saint Petersburg, Trieste's past is for Magris that of a city born of will and artifice, where trafficking replaces the spirit. Yet, Magris admits, in more recent times the hybrid blood of Trieste's ethnic and cultural melting pot has also made the city itself an Orient Express, a Western-Balkanic graft, the Eastern "porta" ("Trieste" 56) [gate] through which an unknown Europe would gain access to Italy, connecting the Latin world to Mitteleuropa.

It could be argued that, if Magris's Trieste is a "porta," it is so not only in the sense of "gate" but also as a domestic "door," which offsets the alienating effect of the city with the warmth and coziness of its coffee houses and taverns, where to move from one table to another is tantamount to exiting one epoch, through an invisible temporal door, and enter another one, but without ever losing the feeling of familiarity. The evident "disconnection" (52) of this spatio-temporal experience synthesizes for Magris the disconnection of the world as a whole, and the intentionally disjointed style with which art represents it. "The city is a place, a center of meaning, par excellence" (Tuan *Space* 173), Tuan claims. In addition to having many symbols, the city itself symbolizes a man-made order and represents the "ideal human community" (173). Yet the subject in Magris's narrative feels at home in disorder, among "those scattered paraphernalia of time" ("Trieste" 52) that furnish his fragmentary urban space. Magris consolidates this experience of homeliness in instability when he explicitly portrays Trieste as "a nomad and fugitive abode" (56) whose dwellers confront the ephemeral multiplicity of things and life's free, anarchic flow. Nourished by the thought of leading intellectuals of Central European modernity like Schopenhauer, Nietzsche, and Freud, Magris's Trieste appears on the twentieth-century cultural scene when the authenticity of life begins to be associated with the consciousness of aging, and truth unmasks the inconsistency of its own foundations by unveiling itself in decline and death. The soul of Trieste, for Magris, is the essence of this irreconcilable contradiction whereby knowledge consists of the awareness and the intensification of one's own downfall. At the same time, however, although this truth uncovers how "discomfort" (59) has decreed the end of stability and permanence, Magris ultimately associates "triestinità" with rootedness in that apparent identitarian exile, and upholds the coexistence of estrangement and integration.[4]

Precisely because—as we will read in *Microcosms*—Trieste is "everything and its opposite" (*Microcosms* 250), Magris's overall works address both the productive and the destabilizing effects of his city's spatio-temporal discontinuity and marginality. On the one hand, Trieste's frontier identity provides the guarantee of openness that Magris discusses in *Utopia e disincanto* in terms of ability to accept boundaries as we do with those of our own dwelling, yet avoiding both the stiffening and the dissolution of identity. On the other hand, borderline Triestness also translates into the estranging experience of fragmentation and of domestic non-belonging that, in Magris's short play *La mostra* [The Exhibition] (2001), marks the self and the life of painter Vito Timmel. From his multicultural roots to the derangement of his mental breakdown,[5] Magris's Timmel embodies the most distinctive and contradictory features of his town, a crossroads of languages and dialects yet enclosed in its decenteredness, culturally and ethnically plural yet also a site of alienation, which in Timmel's case, leads to confinement in a psychiatric hospital.

From the intimacy, protection, and rootedness of the home—albeit temporary—*La mostra* plunges us into the identitarian dissociation inside Timmel's asylum. Here fragmentation does not foster the enrichment that in Magris's "Trieste" derived from the plurality of paraphernalia composing the identitarian mosaic. Rather, it disassembles and ultimately annihilates the self through a process of dismemberment that the play visually introduces with the division of the scene into three different sites simultaneously present on stage: Timmel's grave at the cemetery, the "Paradiso" tavern, and the psychiatric hospital ward. The play's destabilizing spatial multiplicity violates the protected space of personal intimacy and of self-consistency. It stages, on the one hand, Timmel's loss of individual freedom behind the oblong glasses and the iron bars of the asylum cell, and, on the other, the merciless exposure of his privacy by the asylum director, who disrespectfully discloses Timmel's medical records. This parcelization that disassembles the protagonist of *La mostra* in a myriad inauthentic and irreconcilable identities down to his total disintegration occurs, as in *Stadelmann*, through a distortion of reassuring familiar places—in this specific case precisely those of the Triestine urban space that in other works Magris presents as promoters of continuity, like cafés and taverns, as we have seen and as will also emerge in subsequent chapters.

The transient and uninhabitable nature of the places in *La mostra* are further underlined by the frequent references to mortality in the claims of Timmel's friend, Sofianopulo,[6] and reinforced by the looming presence of trespass represented by the cemetery on stage. Frequent quotations from Baudelaire—the poet of temporality *par excellence*—inscribe in the self the mark of ephemerality—"C'est la Mort qui console, hélas!" (*Mostra* 12) [It is Death that consoles, alas!]—of wandering and exclusion—embodied by the errant and exiled albatross in Baudelaire's eponymous poem—and ultimately of a perverse coexistence of existential caducity and moral fallenness, as the crisis that makes Timmel precipitate from the alleged "paradise" (39) of a prelapsarian youth to his "saison en enfer" (49) [season in hell] decrees that "doing is innocence; being is sin and an endless fall" (39).

Sofianopulo's further reference to a "famous hotel" (14) in his recollection of a moment of camaraderie with Timmel brightened up by drinking and eating together introduces an additional site of transit, the hotel, which James Clifford has defined "a place you pass through, where the encounters are fleeting, arbitrary" (*Routes* 17). In the case of *La mostra* we could even claim what Clifford, endorsing Fredric Jameson's standpoint in *Postmodernism, or the Cultural Logic of Late Capitalism*, writes about an icon of postmodernist architecture, the Hotel Bonaventure in Downtown Los Angeles, namely, that the hotel and the other soulless substitutes of the home in the drama of Timmel's life materialize "a confusing maze of levels [that] frustrates continuity" (*Routes* 17) and hence represent the objective correlative of the protagonist's alienation. Timmel is at once mobile and captive, a "Wanderer in the madhouse" (*Mostra* 35), who, "locked in his cell, wanders through paths and marinas" (35), confined in his "autistic dialogue" (35), always in a corner with no interest in other inmates. However, it is as though here Magris intended to depict not only his vision of individual identity but also the collective condition of "triestinità" as an archipelago, where different cultures and ethnicities remain "isolated and closed to one another" (Magris and Ara, *Trieste* 9). Indeed, other psychiatric patients in the chorus of *La mostra* avow that they, too, have experienced Timmel's destabilizing mix of confinement and wandering, each shut up in their own singularity: "In the asylum, while smoking two cigarettes you can emigrate from the Calm ward to the Agitated ward" (*Mostra* 51). Their shared deranged imagination dilates that short walk into a recurring "journey" (52) back and forth, an oscillation between virtual departures and returns, all culminating with a homecoming into insanity.

Whereas in the reassuring coziness associated with the domestic environment the individual sees a promise of self-consolidation and emotional enrichment through human connections, the hotel, the tavern, and the asylum that frame Timmel's life do not promote personal interaction and intercultural knowledge but rather increase the sense of separation and fragmentation, lacerating the stage with the clash of incompatible opposites. If, as we have seen, Trieste turns time into space, the time of Timmel's recollections and dreams in *La mostra* becomes a hallucinatory topography that exasperates De Certeau's distinction between place as the orderly and stable reign of the "proper" (*Practice* 117) and space as a tangle of "intersections of mobile elements" (117). The exhibition of Timmel's works as windows into the convoluted architecture of the painter's psyche enacts expropriation as the only possible existential condition. Conceived as "a labyrinth" (*Mostra* 24), it leads spectators into the "polyhedric systems" (35) of decontextualized and recontextualized signs in Timmel's drawings and obsessions, "meticulous and elementary tangles of architectures, swarming of bricks, mazes of streets and hedges, (…) high brick walls, empty cities, (…) taverns that look like prisons" (34). If for Bachelard "the house shelters daydreaming, (…) [and] allows one to dream in peace" (*Poetics* 6), in *La mostra* even the rare glimpses of tender domestic recollections and dreams[7] are imbued with anguish and loss, consolidating the oppressive effect of "houses like closed drawers, room interiors with barred windows as in lagers" (*Mostra* 43). The fond albeit nostalgic memories of his deceased spouse, here transfigured as the mythological Greek princess Alcestis, carry him away toward the "empty rooms" (58) of an imaginary "royal palace" (58) that his bereavement renders too heartrending to inhabit. If the home cannot offer snugness and protection, Timmel the mental wanderer wants to "jump over the wall" (43). He yearns to overcome barriers and limits because these boundaries are not the porous frontiers offering the enriching chance to merge with otherness, but, rather, impassable, asphyxiating confines that only the wish-fulfilling faculty of this characters' deranged imagination can abate: "domestic walls corroded by the spit of time, high walls, but walls collapse, the sea sweeps them away, crumbles them like a giant cannonball" (44). Sadly, however, beyond the real wall in Timmel's life there is no sea ready to welcome him, but, rather, "an immense abyss" (72).

In this chasm where fall, fallenness, and transience converge, the language of *La mostra* launches a powerful, dramatic echo through the multiple idioms and registers juxtaposed in Timmel's profile as in a cubist portrait: Italian, German, Triestine dialect, some Latin and French, ranging from the bureaucratic to the scurrilous, from the lyric to the scholarly and the normative medico-scientific jargon. The language of the play does not stage the inspiring melting pot of the elite concept of Triestine multiculturalism, but, rather a destructive heteroglossia that assembles and disassembles the debris of a crumbling identitarian edifice. The nomad and fugitive abode that had earlier connoted Trieste is now a Babelic Heideggerian house of being that exposes its cracks and its broken equilibria.

Time and space in *La mostra* become progressively rarefied. Moments go away, "like a headache" (72), between memory and delirium, "forgetting and remembering" (54). Places, too, dissipate. And, as if pushing to the limit Magris's notion of identity by subtraction, the self dissolves as well, a self so unsettled that it cannot even find comfort in the fantasy of freedom. It is so sad to be free, Timmel avows, because to overcome the compact identity[8] imposed on Timmel by constricting categories means to remain "without a name" (74), hence without a dwelling place in the symbolic realm.

Significantly, it is precisely with this experience of loss—loss of a fixed identity, home, and homeland—that Magris begins his narrative itinerary as a fiction writer. Peter Krasnov, the protagonist of Magris's 1984 short novel *Illazioni su una sciabola* [*Inferences from a Sabre*], is the prototypical geographical and mental homeless and deserter that Magris has associated with the Triestine condition. Like Timmel, Krasnov accompanies his spatial displacement with the drifting of his thoughts, across real and virtual places at once familiar and unknown, searching for a dwelling, a space of belonging. Yet, like Timmel, he is condemned to not obtaining it.

2.2 *Inferences from a Sabre*: mapping the heart's homestead

The topos of the provisional domestic walls that surround the private site of the self as much as geographic, cultural, and political landscapes has blended those two dimensions in Magris's poetics since *Inferences from a Sabre*. In this story, an elderly priest, Don Guido, recollects and meditates on the occupation of the North-Eastern borderline Italian region of Carnia during the Second World War by the Germans allied with the Cossacks. The focus of the entire text are open questions about Cossack leader Peter Krasnov, a former Lieutenant General of the Russian army during the 1917 Revolution who later became a leader of the counterrevolutionary White movement and left Russia for Germany. The Germans assured the Cossacks they would be assigned a state, somewhere in the Soviet Union, yet, after the allies' retreat from Russia, this promised land ended up coinciding with a very improbable area, Carnia, in the Italian Friuli region, suddenly transformed into a makeshift micro-nation blending Russian prisoners and exiled Whites headed by Krasnov. On the basis of yet another fallacious promise—the guarantee that they would be handed over to the Russian—the Cossacks ultimately surrendered to the English only to find themselves in Soviet hands, facing trial and execution in their own original homeland or drowning themselves to avoid that lot.

Through Don Guido's retrospective glance at those events, Magris lingers on the fabulations and forgeries of truth that human beings are ready to accept when the homeland ideal reaches radical extremes. He focuses on the figure of Krasnov, who, despite many lost battles, persists in his illusory search for authenticity at the price of a double betrayal: "First of all the Cossacks came to acquire a homeland by robbing others of theirs, but then this desire for authenticity became something false (…) because there was nothing more bogus than a Cossack homeland between Trieste and Udine" (Magris "Self" 15). Just as Krasnov's connivance with fascism perverts his dream of authenticity into its "counterfeit" (15) copy, it is a fake historical premise that triggers Magris's narrative, namely, the belief that Krasnov died in fact while he was fleeing, killed by the Italian Partisans, and that his remains are those of an unknown soldier, found on the banks of a Carnian river together with fragments of a sabre.

Already in the title, the notion of inference—"illazione," an arbitrary supposition not supported by proofs—refers not only to the multiple and conflicting conjectures about the sabre that unearths this little known yet complex episode of Cossack and Italian history. It applies, more extensively, to the speculative conceptualization of individual and collective identity alike, from an individual's home to a people's national homeland or even the longed-for exclusive, communal dwelling place that the nationalistic concept of *Heimat* founds upon a mythical, lost past. The speculative quality of the narrative interrogates univocal perspectives and the solidity of truths, inscribing its historical reconstruction under the aegis of mobility and uncertainty. Arguably, this fictional narrative depicts as much "the experience of a border, lost and found" ("Self" 14) as that of a homeland, found and lost.

The book opens with a home as the cradle for personal memories, a rest-home from which Don Guido offers his testimony of the tragically absurd Cossack occupation of his region. Just as that "improbable" (*Inferences* 7) Cossack Carnia represents a domestic, homely space violated by a foreign presence, the "small but comfortable" (9) room in the rest-home that fosters Don Guido's past reminiscences and current reflections is also attacked by external forces, by the desire to trespass boundaries and life itself: "The world these days fits tightly round me, like shrunken clothes; I'm surrounded by limits—including the blue of the sea and the red of certain evenings on the sea's horizon: enchanting limits, (...) but limits nonetheless. And I am weary, I would like to leave, to cross to the other side" (9). "House everywhere but nowhere shut in" (Bachelard *Poetics* 62) is the motto of Bachelard's "dreamer of dwellings" (62), for whom, whenever "the day-dream of inhabiting is thwarted" (62), the prospect of an "elsewhere should be left open" (62). Don Guido's scanty gatherings with a few friends at a table of the Caffè San Marco make him feel that "we are at home" (*Inferences* 12), yet once again this nook of familiarity becomes a threshold, "between awareness of being and loss of being" (*Poetics* 58) as Bachelard would claim, insofar as from this enclosed space of intimacy he overcomes the limits of his body and his memory, spanning with his recollections from past to future without restraint, all in an eternal present.

Don Guido himself reinforces the connection between the two dwelling places, home and homeland, the spheres of private and public history. He acknowledges that the Cossack occupation of Carnia intersected with his personal life as though it contained his own most authentic history and were the mirror of his own existence. And when we delve into the form and content of the Cossack's episode as it is perceived and related by Don Guido, the implications of this parallel become apparent. Significantly, although Don Guido refers to his account of the historical episode, he never provides us with the actual text of his report. He simply talks about it, without ever giving us direct access to the original written document he produced. Representation replaces and alters facts, and, after surmising that the Cossack officer he had met was Krasnov, he deliberately acknowledges that Krasnov's picture does not coincide with the features of the person he had described in his account. He progressively questions the construction of his own narrative, just as he discovers mysterious and inconsistent details on Krasnov's death that increased "the uncertainty of a period which is already so fragmented" (18).

As he elaborates on the events associated with the recognition of the unknown soldier's body exhumed after 12 years' burial under a wooden cross, Don Guido avows that he is not looking for the truth but rather for "the reasons and explanations" (24) of a forgery of truth,[9] hence implying that a univocal and definitive pronouncement on the actual chain of events is far more improbable and untenable than multiple constructions about it. Therefore, when, after being officially identified, the body finally seems to obtain a name and a tomb, hence a symbolic home offering stability and consistency, the sabre that is also unearthed nearby and ascribed to the alleged Krasnov stands only for a "brief illusion of security" (23) against loneliness "in the flux of things" (22), and in the endless search for an ungraspable truth. Indeed, other documents mentioned in the story promptly refute this association, adding other suppositions. The task of the historian itself thus becomes to reconstruct not so much facts as their distortion, to inquire into the unavoidable resistance that falsification posits to truth, and to acknowledge that one's own discursive production participates in that network of conflicting narratives. Don Guido's own inferences soon begin to clash with the deductions of another character, Doctor Puchta. Likewise, the earlier profile of Krasnov as the defender of discipline and symmetry against pluralism and confusion is at odds with what Zorzut, the former sacristan of the village of Verzegnis where the Cossacks settled, later allegedly claims about Krasnov's actual attraction for "the picturesque disorder of his own motley troops, whose only true military unity consisted in the individual Cossack" (36).

Therefore, the interpretation that Zorzut offers of Krasnov's fidelity to the blade of his sabre as a celebration of temporality—"A splendour of transience shone from that blade—a splendour which the *Atamàn*, of course, never betrayed" (33)[10]—ends up being in unison with Don Guido's own meditations on the dangers of habitual, mechanical repetition, arguably another endorsement of openness to change and transitoriness. In this framework, also the remarks on Krasnov's political design highlight new implications in addition to the tragic repercussions on

Carnia's own destiny and identity. Don Guido begins to think of Krasnov in contradictory terms, as a legitimist patriot who, however, by accepting the German's imposition, agrees to oppress the people of Carnia depriving them of their own homeland, treating *Heimat* and cultural identity as nothing more than temporary homes: "as though it were possible to change the ground beneath the turf that his horses were trampling, or even to level the mountains of Carnia, if not actually to transform them into the expanse of the steppe" (34).

As multiple intentional and involuntary betrayals overlap—the Cossacks' high treason of their own country and the Germans' devious manipulation of the Cossacks coupled with the ruthless exploitation of Carnia—the idea of homeland as a stable geographic and emotional symbolic space turns into the odyssey of the search for it, the hypothetical object of a quest that Krasnov draws on different maps as "a perpetual flight" (56) across numerous territories. "A homeland has its landmarks" (Tuan *Space* 159), Tuan writes. "These visible signs serve to enhance a people's sense of identity; they encourage awareness of and loyalty to place" (159). In Krasnov's case, these markers of individuality and national belonging are shifting fantasies. "He pointed out places, sketched boundaries, (...) fixed imaginary points in that space which he intended to transform into a Cossack homeland" (33).

Evoking Benedict Anderson's remarks about the role of the map as the creator, rather than a product of, collective national identity, its geography and legitimacy (*Imagined* 164), Don Caffaro's recollection of Krasnov's strategies also transcend Anderson's implications. In addition to confirming the notion of nation-ness as imagined community, hence as construction rather than as a natural sense of belonging, here individual and national identity are not only *virtual*, but also *mutable* artifacts. The homeland constantly displaced on the map is precisely a temporary, provisional dwelling place. And the most authentic yet shocking sign of the transience affecting the notion of personal or collective home comes from Don Guido's remarks about houses in light of the tragic, violent epilogue of Krasnov's complicity with German violence. Remembering the debris of the dwellings burnt down by the German and guarded by the Cossacks, Don Guido thinks that "every house is a familiar space patiently carved out of the universal void" (*Inferences* 58), but the Cossacks, who had supposedly settled there "to build themselves a house and to take shelter from the indeterminacy of nothingness" (58) had instead "destroyed the hospitable order enclosed by these walls and delivered it back to formlessness" (58). Krasnov himself seems to embody the fragile, inconsistent, and virtual nature of national identity, insofar as he appears as a copy of the characters of his own books—a "papery creature" (59), who performs in life an "involuntary, papery fate" (59).

There is hence a double irony in Krasnov's situation: despite his religious faith, the Cossack officer does not seem sensitive to the reconciliation that faith encourages between the power of the infinite and the "grateful and affectionate sense of our own finitude" (62). According to Don Guido, Krasnov cannot grasp this paradox because "he himself was an aspect of that irony" (62). Connecting the personal and the political sphere, Krasnov's unconsciously ironic identity reemerges in his conversations with Don Caffaro, when his alleged defense of order and tradition, according to Zorzut, in fact lays bare a rebellious and wandering spirit celebrating "the quick and fleeting victories of the horsemen; the rootless nomads' stark and ephemeral homes; the impulse which fades away and is lost" (64). This hymn to transience—which the emblematic title of one of Krasnov's works, *Everything passes*, well epitomizes—finds its ultimate material correlative in the tent, Krasnov's most authentic homeland and state because, as a temporary dwelling, literally and metaphorically without foundations, it embodies the nomadism to which this rootless character aspires.

When, at the end of Don Guido's account, the image of the broken haft returns, its attribution to Krasnov sounds less obvious, but for this reason no less poignant. It is precisely the uncertainty about its origins and the marks of time that make it more authentic because they synthesize what for Don Guido are the crucial principles of existence and of identity. Symptomatically, Don Guido's final association of the sabre with the memory of a dead tree trunk, decomposed but still recognizable from within the soil that embraces it warmly and maternally, reaffirms the reassuring tenderness of a protective, eulogized, homely space, but does so once again in the framework of its inexorably provisional nature, reflecting upon the brevity of life and the small resistance that can be opposed to it.

Magris, therefore, inaugurates his fictional production with the idea of home locatable only in the very search for it, either as an abode within ourselves or as a land that one never possesses but rather leaves or seeks—a mobile space constantly displaced between the memory and the promise of an illusory dwelling, as in the Cossacks' case. As sociologist Zygmunt Bauman writes in response to Alfred De Musset's claim that "great artists have no country" (*Liquid* 204), instead of endorsing homelessness "the trick is to be at home in many homes, to be in each inside and outside at the same time, to combine intimacy with the critical look of an outsider, involvement with detachment (...) Learning the trick is the chance of the exile" (207). Provisional, unstable, yet indestructible, it is this intimate space of affective identification and sharing that nourishes Magris's idea of travel as an experience of expatriation and fragmentation which however discloses "new homelands of the heart" (*Infinito* xxvii) earlier unknown to the traveler himself.

This attempt to reconcile self-estrangement with rootedness, exile with domesticity, is the focus of Magris's earlier study on the experience of the Jews of the diaspora, *Lontano da dove* [Far from Where], where an interrogation on the idea of departure and distance prompts the eponymous repartee "Far from where?" to imply that the individual deprived of a veritable homeland is never bereaved of his/her own core of recollections and emotions. The Ulysses of the *shtetl*—the small Eastern European Jewish communities that Magris analyzes in Joseph Roth's works (*Lontano* 27)—who moves westward in search of home and homeland does not find Ithaca, but his *nóstos* takes place as a ritual of memory and piety. From Roth's claim that by burying one's father in foreign ground one obtains citizenship rights in that alien land, Magris draws the possibility of owning a homeland in one's heart, and of carrying it along in one's own wandering. But for Krasnov there is neither Ithaca nor *nóstos*. The burial of the unknown soldier in the Carnian soil is not enough to grant the Atamàn and his Cossack army literal and symbolic citizenship in their makeshift Italian homecountry. As a sort of poetic justice, in retaliation for their alliance with the rapacity of German nationalism, after taking homeland away from other people, he and the Cossack community are condemned to uprootedness without the emotional surrogate of a homeland of the soul.

Significantly, however, the "illazioni" in Magris's first fictional work remain central to the national and transnational European questions that Magris develops in his subsequent, much acclaimed *Danube*, *Microcosms*, and *Blindly*, which, against ideological fanaticism, approach identity in an open, speculative way, as a constant process of dislocation which, far from absolute drifting, should rather be conceived as a relocation to a new home—never the same but each time providing temporary comfort.

Notes

1. See, for instance, Dupré *Epica*; Ciccarelli "Crossing."
2. For a more extensive discussion of the role of the café as a temporary home, see Chapter 4.
3. For Magris and Ara this paradoxical condition emerges, in particular, from Franco Vegliani's novel *La frontiera* (107) but their overall argumentation pertains to "triestinità" in more general terms. To be sure, the complexity of the city's history substantiates this connotation. It suffices to think of the condition of Trieste as a contested territory between the Allies and the Yugoslavs in 1945, and as a sort of nowhere land when, at the end of the Second World War, the city became a "free territory" under the UN, but split into two areas, zone A under British and American jurisdiction and eventually handed over to Italy in 1954 after a referendum, and zone B under Yugoslavia until it was annexed to Italy in 1954. It was not until 1975, however, that the situation of the borders with Yugoslavia and of Italian and Slovene minorities in the two nations was settled. For a historical overview of Trieste's paradoxical status, see Schächter *Origin* 5–36.
4. The idea of feeling at home in Trieste's fragmentary cultural geography is also the underlying principle of the 2011 exhibition "The Trieste of Magris" at the Centre de Cultura Contemporànea de Barcelona, where the city is reconstructed through portions of Magris's own dwelling and works, and experienced as a juxtaposition of scenes, materials, and media.
5. Vito Timmel was born in 1886 in Vienna, the son of the German nobleman Raphael von Thümmel and of Friulian Countess Adele Scodellari, and moved to Trieste in 1890. After studying art both in Trieste and in Vienna, he abandoned formal art education and began experimenting with different styles, shifting from Italian *verismo* to German post-impressionism and symbolism (particularly influenced by Klimt and Hodler). With time, Timmel emphasized the symbolist aspect of his aesthetics. With the progressive decline of his mental health, his landscapes and scenes became fantastic and surreal, and, parallel to his pictorial activity, he annotated equally evocative impressions in his journal, *Magico Taccuino*. He died at Trieste's psychiatric hospital in 1949.

   In *La mostra* Magris reinforces the protagonist's estrangement by building his story precisely upon this double representative filter, insofar as he stages Timmel not simply as a historical figure but also as the character that Timmel creates in his own autobiographical account. Timmel already appears in the reminiscences of the narrator of *Microcosms*, as a regular at Caffè San Marco and the probable artist of one of the masks. (*Microcosms* 4–5).

6 Cesare Sofianopulo, another Triestine painter and a friend of Timmel's.
7 "son entrado in una casa e go trovado una dona...(...) ierimo nel paradiso e parlavimo del mondo" (42) [I entered a house and I found a woman...(...) we were in heaven and talked about the world]; "by the sea—right, I was asleep in a strange house" (45). For the first quotation, I have kept the original phrase next to the English translation to provide an instance of the destabilizing effect produced by the shift from standard Italian to Triestine dialect in Timmel's statements throughout the play. *La mostra* has been translated in several European languages—German, Spanish, French, Slovenian—but not yet in English.
8 For Magris "identità compatta" (*Utopia* 60) is what the grim guardians of the frontiers of the self persist in protecting.
9 The Italian original included "una contraffazione della verità" (*Illazioni* 23), which is not present in the English translation. This choice neglects a crucial aspect of Magris's poetics, precisely that of building imaginatively rather than simply representing historical and biographical facts.
10 The term designates the supreme military commander of the Cossack army in the Russian Empire.

3
European Thresholds and Relocations

Abstract: *In his essays on Mitteleuropa, Magris expresses his critical view on the European historical and cultural legacy and on the role of literature as a connection between past and present models of Europeanness. Deprived of a unitary center and of grand syntheses, the dislocated Mitteleuropean subjectivity defends marginality and transience against totalizing designs, and provides the background for Magris's exploration of the European consciousness in terms of identitarian and cultural relocation in* Danube. *Through a comparison of Magris and Zygmunt Bauman's conceptions of liquidity and community, the chapter analyzes images of provisional dwellings in* Danube, *showing how Magris makes domestic intimacy coexist with the uncertainty of a life in progress, and reconceives borders as thresholds. People are truly at home not when they remain enclosed within their domestic walls, but rather when they move toward new dwellings, questioning identity as aggressive assertion of self-sameness.*

Keywords: borders and diversity; *Danubio [Danube]*; Europe; liquidity; Mitteleuropa; Zygmunt Bauman

Pireddu, Nicoletta. *The Works of Claudio Magris: Temporary Homes, Mobile Identities, European Borders.* New York: Palgrave Macmillan, 2015.
DOI: 10.1057/9781137488046.0006.

3.1 Mitteleuropa: a dislodged center

> One feels at home, in Europe, and in one of the airiest rooms of our common European home. (Magris *Infinito* 26)

The feeling of homeliness extolled in this opening quotation condenses Magris's impressions about a place paradoxically situated at the extreme margins of Europe, namely, the Canary Islands, politically Spanish but geographically much closer to Africa. Despite its decentralized location, however, this archipelago suggests a connection with a paramount topic in Magris's historical and cultural reflection, namely, the Europeanness of Danubian civilization. The Canaries, in his view, seem to be even closer to his European ideal than the area of Central Europe to which Magris has devoted numerous works, because, despite their insularity, they have overcome the obsessive fixation with their own identity. The openness to the world and the cosmopolitan familiarity that Magris finds in the small archipelago, with its vibrant intellectual life extending well beyond their insular borders despite frequent claims to political autonomy, confirm that islands and coasts are often less isolated and closed in on themselves than places located on land (*Infinito* 27). The journey to the extreme southern and western boundaries of Europe is hence also an occasion for Magris to address the identitarian issue in the borderline areas that have shaped his life and writing, namely, the uncertain and composite Mitteleuropean countries. Be it in the case of the peripheral European islands at the border with Africa or of the nations in the heart of the Old Continent, Magris engages with the difficult balance between cultural unity and respect of diversity, underlining that defense of one's own identity should not overlook the existence of a higher sphere of belonging, which, in his cultural vision, corresponds above all to the European dimension.

Considered *the* contemporary Mitteleuropean writer and scholar of Mitteleuropa by definition, Claudio Magris has been associated with the idea of Mitteleuropa since 1963, the publication year of his *Il mito absburgico nella letteratura austriaca moderna* [The Hapsburg Myth in Modern Austrian Literature], a seminal text which has contributed to the redefinition of a literary and cultural category, and, in Italy, even to its creation. Magris has frequently defined this book as an autobiographical essay[1] for its deep connection with the places, traditions, and ideas that converge into his personal Triestine history and that inspire the entirety of his subsequent literary production. But, above all, and intertwined with the autobiographical vein, Magris's fascination with Danubian civilization leads him in this book to revise the deforming image of the Austro-Hungarian reality, and of its literature and culture in particular, deriving from the mythization of the Hapsburg world. Aiming to transcend both the acritically celebratory approach to the Mitteleuropean search for order and unity and the equally tendentious denigration of its discovery of fragmentation and chaos, Magris presents the Hapsburg world as the symbol of a crumbling totality, and its literature as an odyssey among those fragments (*Mito* 7). At the same time, however, he attempts to defend what for him is the sense of totality in the world and in history. Against the stereotypical negative depiction of Austrian literature as a disenchanted expression of loss and nihilism, Magris still upholds the quest for meaning, even in a Babelic world.

As Magris explains on several occasions—for instance in his essay "Mitteleuropa: Reality and Myth of a Word"—the concept of Mitteleuropa does not overlap with the idea of "Central Europe," although they seem to have the same meaning. A very controversial term, Central Europe refers to a predominantly geographical notion, and, especially after the Second World War, a geopolitical one, generally associated with countries like Poland, Czechoslovakia, or Hungary, mainly communist states with cultural ties to Western Europe.[2] For its part, Mitteleuropa connotes a wider cultural area that also includes Austria and Germany and that hence, for Magris, implies certain unifying historical, political, and cultural elements shared by cities like Vienna, Trieste, Berlin, Budapest, Zagreb, and Krakow "despite great differences, tensions, and conflicts" ("Mitteleuropa" 141) and the difficulties tracing their boundaries. Foregrounding the malleability, ambivalence, if not vagueness, of the Mitteleuropean idea, Magris explains that the historical origins of the term often clash with its literary reverberations. Yet, the focus of his investigation is the intersection of those two domains, where also the principles emerge of his vision of the European cultural identity and of Europe's present and future possibilities.

Analyzing different writers' perceptions of Mitteleuropa, from Urzidil and Slataper to Werfel, Musil, and Roth among many others, Magris emphasizes the *leitmotif* of its abstract and indefinable nature, "its irreducibility to any overly precise identity" ("Mitteleuropa" 142), its "protean" (142) quality defying univocal labels. Through the mingling and overlapping of nations, and the "perpetually changing, growing" (142) Mitteleuropean identity, always on the verge of loss, Magris seems to prefigure the pluralism of his imagined Europe-to-come. However, he does not intend to revive geographical and historical terms of comparisons to adopt them acritically for the present or future. Nostalgia makes us look back to a spatial and temporal stability that, as Tuan claims, makes us feel "proprietary about things" (*Space* 188) by evoking "an idealized and stable past" (188). For his part, although Magris considers nostalgia a necessary experience for self-knowledge, he does not uphold the past as a value in itself.[3] He strongly relies on memory as a provider of continuity in passions and sentiments, but rejects the obsessive "false memory" (Obrist and Magris) that renders us prisoners of the past.

As he writes in the book that he designates as the continuation of *Il mito absburgico*, namely, *L'anello di Clarisse* [Clarisse's ring], although it is true that the Austrian decenteredness depicted by the Hapsburg myth results from a radical historical crisis that can symbolize the unreality of Europe as a whole (*Clarisse* 59), one should not take that fantastic semblance for a concrete truth. In other words, historical reality should never be mystified by rhetorical assertions. Magris hence recognizes that Mitteleuropean pluralism has often been reduced to "a chaotic Babel" ("Mitteleuropa" 143) or nostalgically extolled as a folkloric phenomenon without a deep knowledge of or balanced approach to its complexity. Drawing attention to the contrast between the two main connotations of the notion of Mitteleuropa, namely, the cosmopolitan, intellectual ideal attached to the last phase of the Hapsburg empire and the Prussian conception of Mitteleuropa based upon Germany's hegemony over other Danubian nationalities, he underlines their respective stereotypes, namely, the alleged unity under the House of Hapsburg, and, at the same time, the degeneration of the pan-Germanic design into the devastating epilogue of National Socialism.[4]

Blending elements from both these conceptions, Magris in a more recent article in *Corriere della sera* synthesizes Mitteleuropa as a multilingual and multicultural mosaic traversed by common elements underlying national differences ("Terza alba" 39). Without denying the role of the Hapsburg empire in this allegedly shared cultural setting, he points at two paramount supranational unifying factors—the German language spoken in all the non-German countries of that world and the Jewish civilization present in each of them. Mitteleuropa, Magris concludes, hence stood for a humanistic ideal, the sense of belonging to a wider culture than any national identity. As Magris further elaborates in his earlier essay, the common feature of most representations of Mitteleuropa is the perception that "the liberal imperative and the imperative of the state (in the modern sense) intersect with the imperative of respecting not only national cultural and political particularisms, but also the so-called historical rights of national or social groups, or local hierarchies, customs, traditions and authorities" ("Mitteleuropa" 145). In these premises we see an intimation of Magris's approach to the political and cultural identity of the contemporary Europe in progress, a polycentric and non-hierarchical conception which can be explained in terms of Jürgen Habermas's "postnational constellations" (*Postnational* 88), a network of parallel horizontal allegiances in a self-steering, democratic European reconfiguration.[5]

For Magris, the search for and awareness of a common Mitteleuropean legacy also establishes a unity which, even if it did not exist in the past, nourishes the sense of a shared heritage in the present or future. His argument thus corroborates the productivity of the virtual, fictional dimension in the nation-building process discussed for instance by Anderson through his notion of imagined community, which Magris's European outlook here extends to the supranational level. Precisely because it is "the realm of the imaginary" ("Mitteleuropa" 147), literature plays a central role in the Mitteleuropean consciousness of belonging to a plural Danubian culture, because it embodies "that which has no existence [yet] except in words" (147), but which "becomes individuated as a force latent in reality, like a chrysalis striving to become a butterfly" (147). Literature, therefore, is "the essence or true face of history" (147), because it is endowed with the potential to realize even what politics has thwarted or distorted. As a committed nineteenth-century Europeanist, Giuseppe Mazzini, already explicitly claimed in his essay "D'una letteratura europea" [For a European literature], literature no longer expresses and follows reality but anticipates and shapes it, and what the present may dismiss as the alleged utopian quality of its virtual world will be called reality as soon as facts will corroborate its truth (Mazzini "Letteratura" 44; 30). Magris, however, does not yield unconditionally to this Romantic vision, and highlights the need to counterbalance utopia with a cautious and measured stance, so as to avoid irrational, totalizing extremes. This is an example of what in *Utopia e disincanto* and in various other works Magris connotes as the coexistence of utopia and disenchantment in his intellectual and ethical vision, with which here he tempers both nihilistic and idyllic approaches to individual and national identities. In the Mitteleuropean condition we thus see a reflection of Magris's own conception of reality, which, like the Danubian civilization emerging from literature, exhibits "the Janus-face of a double truth: the nostalgia for order, and the unmasking of disorder" ("Mitteleuropa" 147). Mitteleuropa, Magris adds, can be considered "a great laboratory of contemporary nihilism and at the same time of an ironic but tenacious resistance to this same nihilism" (147).

For Magris, indeed, Mitteleuropean culture conveys the experience of an ending that perpetually approaches without ever really happening (Magris and Gambaro "Entretien" 102). It deeply feels "the precariousness of individual identity, the fragility of the subject" ("Mitteleuropa" 150) deprived of "a unitary centre synthesizing and ranking contradictions" (150). However, this apparent existential dislocation into a "chaotic and incongruous forum" (150) is also a conceptual relocation, as the inability to conceive grand syntheses or universal principles does not lead to dissolution. Rather, it becomes a defense of "the marginal, peripheral and transient" (150) as a form of "radical critique" (150) of, and even resistance to totalizing, authoritarian designs. Magris's characterization of the Mitteleuropean culture of irony as an instrument of moderation can hence be read as a counterdiscourse to the Eurocentrism of the past but also as a warning against the persisting risks of discrimination and hegemony within Europe itself. Significantly, Magris explains how, after the Second World War, the Mitteleuropean approach "became a way of thinking about another Europe than the one which emerged from Yalta" (151), a Europe cultivating dialogue and mediation, instead of endorsing the oppositional logic of superpowers. Therefore Magris's Mitteleuropa is at once the metaphor for the broken unity of the Western world and the remedy to this fragmentation because its intrinsic pluralism substantiates the possibility of cohesion within multiplicity.

The Mitteleuropean desire for a harmonious collectivity and the simultaneous acknowledgment of a contradictory heterogeneity connote Magris's own approach to the European project, seen precisely as an antidote to the current European crisis.[6] Without neglecting the difficulties affecting national pluralism and multiculturalism both in the Mitteleuropa of the past and in the Europe of the present and future, Magris, however, reiterates that even nowadays Mitteleuropa can help us learn a fundamental analytical tool, precisely "irony (...) towards every historical actuality that announces itself as the only possible reality" (152). In his more recent intervention in *Corriere della sera* Mitteleuropa appears even more assertively as a much needed critical lens and a metaphor of resistance to all totalizing political and philosophical systems that attempt to command the world as an army and to triumphally guide the march of history itself ("Terza alba" 39). Precisely because Mitteleuropean civilization is so sensitive to discontent, so distrustful of the arrogance of progress and so knowledgeable of the fragments and shadows of existence that remain at its margin, Magris concludes that its culture and humanity are all the more necessary to compensate for what the heart is missing.

It is this dialectical approach that we can also grasp in *L'anello di Clarisse*, where the sense of life as a whole shines through "the crack that prevents the whole from closing in a definitive compactness" (*Clarisse* 59) and hence nourishes the ability of life to perpetually become other than itself while remaining loyal to itself. Appropriating Hoffmansthal's reflections, Magris locates the essence of life in the antithesis of faithfulness and metamorphosis, change and duration. The secret is to treat that antithesis as complementarity, so as to live that tension as harmony, insofar as it is through "the void and the absence of definitive conquests" (59) that life reveals its sense, just as the crisis of the word, with its constant process of creation and recreation, founds great style instead of disintegrating it.

Doing and undoing, dislocation and relocation, are precisely the propelling forces of Magris's fictional sequel to his Mitteleuropean critical journey, namely, *Danube*. Magris's narrative of his real and symbolic journey along the Danube—written in 1986 and to date still his most renowned and acclaimed work—retraces the places and the myths of Mitteleuropa while inviting us to reflect, through them, upon the European cultural legacy and the challenges and potentiality of the ongoing European project.

3.2   *Danube*: the liquid path to rooted homelessness

From the treatment of the private, individual self and of the collective urban and national spaces as a moving and mutable abode, Magris, with *Danube*, reconceptualizes Europeanness as a geographical and temporal process of unsettlement and resettlement, in a tension between the local and the global spheres. In line with the hybrid form of Magris's book—at once travelogue, memoir, novel, philosophical treatise, literary and historical essay—the conceptual fluidity of the Austrian and Mitteleuropean river *par excellence* not only undermines the idea of origin as self-sameness but also represents "*the* image for the questioning of identity" (*Danube* 21). Not accidentally, it is the role of liquidity in Magris's book that so far has engaged most critics. What still deserves attention, however, is the fact that the Danube's liquid geography and the inconsistency of the self that it represents are in a symbiotic relationship with the household as a real or symbolic locus of traditions and affections. As the coexistence of stability and mutability, the home in *Danube* exhibits more explicit cultural implications at the national and supranational levels which foreground a "poetics and ethics of Europeanness" (Pireddu "On the Threshold" 334), founded upon the positive value of the temporary abode as a promoter of multiplicity, yet simultaneously as a custodian of geopolitical and ethical limits.

3.2.1 Fluctuating domiciles

The object of a dispute between two towns—Furtwangen and Donaueschingen—negotiating between two toponyms, Donau and Breg, each immortalized in its supposed uniqueness by a plate, the river that intrigues the narrator of *Danube* and many scholars before him is equally enigmatic because of its origin, significantly associated with a house. The old abode with the gutter that according to Amedeo's report coincides with the Danube itself in fact turns out to be, in a more complex way, the site of a conceptual loop according to which the alleged source of the Danube is also the channel that conveys it, simultaneously cause and effect, without the possibility of distinguishing between the two—the gutter and a basin that is "constantly full because of a tap that no one ever succeeds in turning off; and (…) in turn connected to 'a lead pipe, which may well be as old as the house, and which ends up God knows where'" (24). If these initial sketches already underscore the paradoxical, non-teleological nature of the river, in a subsequent inspection the Danubian narrator soon debunks the existence of the tap itself, the supposed connection between the water and its transmission channel. By the same token, the rugged trail toward and around the house mimics the obstacles of this hydrographic quest through the simile that the narrator proposes with the winding route of expression in the case of intellectual or emotional blockages. Just as the house itself for the narrator takes on the quality of an epistolary description where digressions replace the concern with scientific precision and univocity, literary activity becomes a journey made of chinks and tatters, "far from the house where we were born, and from the Promised Land" (26). *Danube* significantly opens precisely with a reflection on "the unpredictability of travel, the intricacy and divergence of paths, the fortuity of delays, the uncertainty of evening and the asymmetrical quality of any journey" (15).

Travel may disassemble landscapes and sceneries. Yet, no matter how disorienting, it always has an architecture to which "it is possible to contribute a few stones" (16). Likewise, literature is not simple dislocation but rather "trasloco" (*Danubio* Garzanti 1990: 15) [relocation],[7] hence it keeps a link with a domestic context to which to go back between displacements.

Reconceptualized as relocation, it loses something as it gives up stability, but also finds something else from forgotten closets (18). For the narrator, this tension between loss and retrieval that characterizes spatial transfer is the very "Statute for Living" (*Danube* 15), and *Danube* displays it since its outset, as it welds together the personal and the collective domains around the precarious condition of temporary dwelling. Transcending the individual's status, the passage "across the face of the earth as guests" (15) also means that "every nation is destined to have its day, and that there are not, in any absolute sense, greater or lesser civilizations, but rather a succession of flowerings" (32–33).

In the absence of an originary foundation, that is, of an identifiable birth house for the Danube—"The gutter which feeds the spring is itself fed by the spring (28)—the interpretive approach to the real and symbolic space traced by the river is precisely the very "illazione" (*Danubio* Garzanti 1990: 27) [inference][8] that accompanied the enigmas of Krasnov's sabre in *Inferences from a Sabre*. Just as conjectures investigated multiple suppositions but never completely unearthed a definitive, univocal truth about the Cossack chief, the Danube—opposed to the Rhine, the "mythical custodian of the purity of the race" (29)[9]—is the meeting point of different peoples, the symbol of a multiple and supranational *koiné*, of a Mitteleuropean Austrian empire that constituted a world behind the nations. To follow the flow of the Danube with Magris means precisely to travel along a tortuous road dotted with geographical and sentimental spaces that test the European ideal through an ongoing confrontation with the hidden agendas behind myths and ideologies. To avoid a facile, essentializing vision of a multicultural European model like the "harmony between different people" (29) simplistically associated with the Hapsburg's vocation, the narrator tries to approach his journey along the river without preconceived ideas, expecting both tensions and more peaceful social interactions. The ironic identitarian approach recurring in Magris's poetics is here presented as a guarantor of tolerance and of openness to the difformities of life, just like the Danube itself comes to symbolize the Austrian acceptance of the world's heterogeneities and contradictions, against the acritical belief in human universals.

Significantly, soon after the narrator endorses Sigmund von Birken's vision of our earthly homeland as the locus of imperfection and precariousness, the first of the many homes that the Danubian traveler visits is that of the young Martin Heidegger, of whom the narrator highlights the dangerous yet enlightening aporias in his view on domestic intimacy. However genuine, the German philosopher's attachment to the most symbolic components of his immediate community (woods, dialect, hearth) for Magris shows the limits of the cult of *Heimat* when it is not tempered by equal consideration for other people's love of their own turf and dwellings—"their log cabins, or their blocked-rent tenements, or their skyscrapers" (45). It is only when he recognizes the need to "leave home far behind" (46) and the existence of "other soils and other lands" (45) that Heidegger can transcend this exclusive "monopoly of authenticity" (45) to which in fact he clings in order to preserve hope in a non-alienated life, protected from what he felt as the depersonalizing effects of modernity. However, meditating upon the symbolic value of that Heideggerian veneration for the abode, be it the home of his youth in Messkirch or the cabin in the Black Forest of his elderly years, Magris observes that Heidegger also refutes the rhetoric of rootedness the moment he understands the necessity of "displacement" (46), the need to "tear up our roots" (46) precisely to be able to grasp and authentically love being and homeland: "without loss and disorientation, without wandering along paths that peter out in the woods, (…) there is no possibility of hearing the authentic word of Being" (46). This paradoxical blend of rootedness and errance synthesizes for Magris not only the experience of identity but also the possibility of a European consciousness precisely as temporary homeliness.

Further progressing along *Danube*, a more traumatic experience of uprooting—that of Louis Ferdinand Céline in the "papier-mâché palace" (*Danube* 53) of Sigmaringen—testifies to the violent destruction of domesticity. "[H]ouses gutted by bombs" (50) are a gruesome reminder of the horrors of a war propelled by racial hate. Against the negative backdrop of this terrifying "epiphany of nothingness" (55), however, the Austrian playwright Franz Grillparzer embodies the constructive potential of the "divided, ambivalent individual" (79), for Magris a powerful protection from ideological totalitarianism. It is this model of irregularity at the individual and collective levels that we also find in Jean Paul's perception of his lack of self-identity and of "the incompleteness and fragmentary nature of reality" (85). This feeling for Magris can depict our condition of inhabitants of a world open to an elsewhere, in which there is no difference between traveling and staying home because moving "between Troy and Ithaca [or] between kitchen and dining-room" (85) implies, nonetheless, being "poised between two worlds" (85). Both stretches are long and take place in a "vast, unknown kindgom" (85), be it the dwelling place within the domestic walls or a real odyssey toward destinations lost beyond the horizon.

In another narrative flash, inside or outside his Linz home overlooking the Danube, Austrian writer Adalbert Stifter looks for small events appropriate to an individual who, in Magris's view, respects the limit of his own personal value in order to leave room to others and to establish a dialogue with them while recognizing their own autonomy. Symptomatically, though, to the calm "epic quality" (130) of Stifter's domestic order there follows the praise of fluidity expressed by Marianne Jung Willemer, Goethe's Suleika, whose native home is commemorated by a plate. Happy to be nothing more than "a passing moment" (132) but "completely at home in a protean, ever-changing life" (132), Suleika's self and the home that remembers her can be seen as the other half of Stifter's simple microcosm of continuity and present. Yet enduring values and memories seem to vacillate when the prevailing approach to life is a "look behind" (206) like that of Otto Weininger who, in the house where Beethoven's days also ended, takes his life, in a lost battle against the "irreversibility of time" (206). On 35 Rembrandtstrasse, from Joseph Roth's gray home, the melancholy and disenchantment caused by transience become the feature of Vienna and of Central Europe as a whole, "the art of living on the brink of nothingness" (193), in "one prolonged epilogue" (193), in search of a symmetry able to elude ephemerality, at least temporarily.

However, it is this very symmetry that, if elevated to the supreme goal of transcending finitude and limits, leads to a "pathetic uselessness" (169).[10] This is what the narrator realizes in front of the ascetic geometric rationality of Ludwig Wittgenstein's home: the philosopher's dwelling raises doubts about the very possibility of "a real house, or what once was called hearth and home" (169) as custodians of the warmth and intimacy of affections. But the narrator's meditations also correct the excesses of Wittgenstein's closed forms and the exclusions they entail. This is Magris's way of underlining the constructive power of limits, which the Mitteleuropean civilization shows whenever it aspires to perfect totality while simultaneously exposing its missing pieces, "the cleavages (...) in every individual and society" (170). A last stop in Vienna, indeed, leads the narrator to define the Austrian capital as "one vast café" (215) precisely because it is at once the locus "of methodical habits and of casual comings and goings" (215). Vienna hence represents not only the reassuring familiarity of an unchanged domestic intimacy but also the unknown within the new, in line with that "vagabond impermanence that is our destiny" (215).

In *L'infinito viaggiare* Magris recalls Viennese philosopher Otto Weininger's pronouncements on the immorality of travel, predicated upon the assumption that a strong "I" has to stay home to face anguish and despair without distraction (*Infinito* xx). Yet for the author of *Danube* what authenticates our humanity is the *dépaysement* of the departure from home, with its alternation of accomplishments and failures. Transit and transience—transit *as* transience—confront us with the unexpected, making us feel like foreigners among other foreigners and in our own home. But it is this experience of estrangement and temporality that brings us together.

3.2.2 Soluble sites

In the temporary domesticity that connotes his European dimension, Magris inscribes his idea of borders and frontiers as thresholds, extending the implications of the house image from individual subjectivity to collective historical memory and to national and supranational consciousness. Franco Cassano asserts that "the frontier does not unify *and* divide, but it unifies *because* it divides" (Cassano *Southern* 43). The etymology of "confine" means "contact, points in common" (44) yet, at the same time, the frontier has its own transgression inscribed in itself. For his part, focusing on the relationship between legitimate space and its alien exteriority in the case of rivers and bridges as particular instances of border ambivalence, De Certeau underscores the "dynamic contradiction between each delimitation and its mobility" (126). Founded upon contrasts, the frontier is a paradoxical site whose "points of differentiations are also their common points" (127). In this tension between conjunction and disjunction, neither of the two bodies in contact owns the frontier. As a frontier itself that eludes appropriation, the river "does not have the character of a nowhere that cartographical representation ultimately presupposes. It has a mediating role" (*Practice* 127). Substantiating Cassano and De Certeau's observations, Magris's river also connects with other borderline conditions in the book,[11] turning them into thresholds that favor cohabitation of self-sameness and alterity.

For instance, the Latin "*Limes*" that surrounded the Roman Empire and of which the narrator follows some sections in his Danubian journey was not only a demarcating line but an attempt at protecting the Roman claim to eternal universality against the backdrop of alleged barbarians who, no longer conquerable, had to be at least kept off. But if "*imperium* is a barrier, a defense, a rampart" (98) against the barbaric "uncouthness of the indistinct and the individualistic" (98), history has shown us that those despised barbarians have in fact become "the artificers of the new Europe" (98). Therefore, in Magris's vision of our Europe as the daughter of that *Limes* we can see the grandiose yet problematic historical heritage of a civilization mainly sensitive to its own primacy and, simultaneously, the awareness of its transience. Each individual and tradition alike has its own hour and mission in history, hence for "every power which claims to represent universality and civilization there comes the time to pay the price, to deliver up its arms to those who a moment before were thought of as uncouth inferiors" (98).

This reflection on a European past characterized by what I would define as Eurocentrism on a global scale, and justified by arbitrary political and cultural hierarchies, also acts as a warning for the present and future of Europe. As we can infer from Magris's essay "Limes. Frontiera dell'essere, cerchio che racchiude," far from diminishing the importance of the European cultural heritage, Magris invites us to come to terms with its most problematic aspects by reappropriating historical memory not so much with visceral idolatry as with critical appreciation of the past's heterogeneity, including the alternative projects that the past did not pursue but that could become potential futures (*"Limes"* 54; 58). More than ever, the complex interactions of different national cultures within Europe corroborates the need to address the contrast between an ideal of balanced pluralism and the still dominant role of specific and allegedly superior cultural expressions. Hence, for instance, if in Hölderlin's times the Germans were considered "the Greeks of the new Europe" (*Danube* 99), that is, the only civilization able to reestablish a universally human culture, contemporary Europe needs to interrogate its own relationship with German leadership. While, in the past of Germany, cultural assimilation often meant a one-way process coinciding with Germanization, in the current and future European scenario integration depends for Magris upon the ability to put aside egocentric particularism and to overcome conflicts of interests (*"Limes"* 72).

Therefore, despite Magris's historiographic appetite and his Danubian traveler's philological and archaeological approach to reality—which renders him a little warrior against oblivion, as Magris defines him in his essay "Danubio e post-Danubio" (25)—*Danube* does not aim at a simple revival of Europe's historical and cultural past. Beyond his criticism of Eurocentrism, as of any geopolitical or ideological center, Magris here shows once again his cautiousness about the very Mitteleuropean model of a pacific and tolerant consortium of nations that seems to inspire his vision of the current Europe-building process. The caveat that applies to the European Union as much as to the Mitteleuropean Danubian culture is the risk of a fortress Europe which, simply in order to differentiate and exclude, shuts itself up behind an impenetrable *Limes* as solid as that of the "frontiersmen" (*Danube* 326) guarding the borders of the Danubian unity, a cluster of "composite and undefined" (327) nationalities solidly bound together by a fierce desire to safeguard their land "against any external authority" (327). Rather than take the Mitteleuropean ideal only as "a great civilization of defensiveness, of barriers thrown up against life (...) to protect oneself from outside attack" (155), the narrator highlights the need to temper it with the epic openness of liquidity as "abandonment to the new and the unknown" (155).

To be sure, the predominant interpretation of *Danube* as a liquid epic connotes the journey along the river at once as an itinerary of liberation from the rigor of constraining categories and as a path fraught with geographical obstacles and intellectual challenges, one of the numerous odysseys in Magris's overall works. Furthermore, with its impetuous flow, the river conveys the idea of temporality, change, and renewal more effectively than the eternal uniformity of the sea. However, through his treatment of liquidity Magris raises additional philosophical and ethical implications for mobility and domesticity, which, for instance, have also systematically marked Zygmunt Bauman's thought. An examination of the two intellectuals' respective approaches to liquidity can hence help us better appreciate the specificity of Magris's contribution.

Through the idea of liquidity, to which he has devoted numerous works, Bauman exposes the increasing uncertainty that affects contemporary life and that modernity attempted to master with rules, hierarchies, and categories able to provide solidity and stability. The liquid individual moves fluidly from one condition to another, deprived of traditional reference points and stable sources of support. For Bauman, the freedom that the liquidity of "an unfixed identity" (*Liquid Life* 32) apparently grants is in fact "not a state of liberty but an obligatory and interminable conscription into a war of liberation that is never ultimately victorious" (32). Bauman's critical approach to liquidity hence treats the culture of extraterritoriality and hybridity as the search for identity in "*non-belonging*" (29), defiance of the borders defining traditional (and allegedly inferior) lives, and desire "to feel everywhere *chez soi*—in order to be vaccinated against the vicious bacteria of domesticity" (29). In the fluid world he depicts, human bonds are subject to a "precariousness" (161) that conceives of objects, experiences, and human beings alike as entities to be consumed and disposed off (*Liquid Modernity* 162–163). In this volatile context of "scattered and wandering emotions" (*Life* 37), therefore, the status of the community itself is "fragile and short-lived" (37), nothing more than the object of a "forever inconclusive search for a secure haven" (37). For Bauman the only possible shareable experience in a liquid society is that offered by "communities of shared worries, shared anxieties or shared hatreds" (37), that is, instances of "a momentary gathering around a nail on which many solitary individuals hang their solitary individual fears" (37). Consequently, the very notion of home, as the image of protective solidity *par excellence* against an alienating liquidity seems to be threatened in Bauman's thought. Dwelling cannot be compatible with the contemporary uncertainty and chaotic instability in which individuals are perpetually "composing, decomposing, recomposing their identities" (*Life* 28).

Against this destabilizing mutability, Bauman, like Magris, supports the essential role of cultural and moral reference points shaped by the shared patrimony of tradition and able to foster change and innovation for and within collectivity: "the memory of the past and trust in the future have been thus far the two pillars on which the cultural and moral bridges between transience and durability, human mortality and the immortality of human accomplishments, as well as taking responsibility and living by the moment" (*Modernity* 129). However, Bauman focuses primarily on the negative effect of mobility and liquidity as causes of a "heterogeneous—and ephemeral, volatile, incoherent, eminently mutable—identity" (*Life* 29). His conception of liquid life, of "a permanently impermanent self, completely incomplete, definitely indefinite—and authentically inauthentic" (33), hence undermines the power of domesticity to offset the radical inconsistency of current social and ethical bonds, as well as flippant intellectual engagement. For his part, as *Danube* shows in an articulated fashion, Magris finds in conceptual fluidity a deterrent against the aggressive assertion of self-sameness, but he does not encroach into the anarchic perpetual becoming that Bauman fears. *Danube* offers a middle ground between the liquidity of experience and the solid locus of memories and affections represented by the household. Synthesizing this coexistence of domestic stability and mutability, Magris maintains that we are not at home when we remain enclosed within our abode, no matter how extended it is, but rather when we move toward new homes, free from the anxiety of having incessantly to confirm our own identity inside the same four walls, and finding our dwelling in the always open-ended sum of the places we have seen.[12] The voyage along the Danube, as Magris has often explained, is, among other things, a journey to overcome Mitteleuropean obsessions ("Danubio e post-Danubio" 28)—in particular the fierce inability to forget the painstaking memory that records everything and that exacerbates the fixation with hyphenated identities.

In the liquid world that Bauman questions, the possibility of unity within the self-asserting communities of "multi-faceted" (*Modernity* 177) individuals depends upon the drawing of "boundaries dividing 'us' from 'them'" (176) along the lines of the allegedly crucial differences that "preclude a common stand and render genuine solidarity unlikely whatever the similarities that make us alike" (176). Significantly, endorsing social anthropologist Fredrick Barth's standpoint, Bauman denounces the artificiality and arbitrariness of such process of separation by stressing that the borders between belonging and non-belonging "do not acknowledge and register the already existing estrangement; they are drawn (...) before the estrangement is brought about" (177). For his part, Magris tries precisely to transcend that arbitrary polarization. In *Danube*, the river exemplifies Magris's reconceptualization of the border as a domestic threshold as it shows the historical and cultural "need and ability to give oneself limits and form" (*Danube* 98) while at the same time it represents a line of contact, epitomizing the productive diversity of that Hapsburg Austria whose anthem would be sung in 11 different languages. On the one hand, it accompanies us into Saxon towns imbued with "a melancholy poetry of orderliness and repetition" (312), a "love of the home" (313) that reveals the need to cling to the stability of habitual places as an illusory duration snatched from an ephemeral existence and history. On the other, it gives us access to the stanzas of Miroslav Krleža, "the poet of the encounter and clash" (253) between all the diverse Danubian peoples, a symbolic domestic world corresponding not so much to a regular, narrow horizon of action as to a Pannonian "melting-pot" (254) where "the individual discovers the plurality, and the uncertainty—though also the complexity—of his own identity" (254).

3.2.3   House, town, community

If, as we often read in *Danube*, the city is an extension of the domesticity of the home, seen as the meeting point of consistency and change, it is not surprising that a city like Belgrade strikes the traveler precisely as "a great forge of metamorphoses" (331), a locus of multiplicity, incessantly renewing itself. This irreducibility to a univocal dimension, which Magris underlines in the habitat of the self and of the other, also characterizes the "composite ethnic substratum" (367) of Bucharest, the "multiple, changing face" (367) of an "ancient amalgam" (367) for which Magris adopts the term "Balkanization" (366). For him, first of all, this expression means imitation of the style and of the way of life of the nineteenth-century European capital *par excellence*, Paris, whose Europeanness is diluted in the Rumanian capital but also revived in a new fashion, merging with and enriching the local ambiance. Yet, the encounter with Eastern European architectural eclecticism is not only an experience of exotic defamiliarization.[13] It also stimulates ethical and political reflections about the uses of diversity. While still in the Serbian town of Subotica, "houses shriek out in notes of blue and yellow, (...) like sea-shells, fretted with decorations and extravagant ornaments, crowns which look like pineapples, *putti* but with enormous breasts, gigantic bearded caryatids whose lower limbs become those of lions, which in turn dissolve in a formless swirl" (323). The narrator elaborates on the city's allegedly fascinating stylistic "falsifications and infractions" (322). As in the *fin-de-siècle* Vienna criticized by Broch, the narrator unmasks a vacuum behind the surface of sequins—the "total lack of values" (323) that enabled the "fakery" (323) of the dreadful Stalinist masquerade of life and of the multiple cover-ups of revolutionaries who "change, multiply, disguise and lose their identities" (323).

Likewise, the heavily ornate Franco-Balkan style in Bucharest appears to him as "hounded by an abhorrence of vacuum" (365) which accentuates the curves of Parisian balconies and wrought-iron decorations amidst the surrounding neglect. Yet the narrator asserts the continuity, rather than the contrast, between the elegant residences and the nearby market stalls selling ill-smelling food and vulgar *bric-à-brac*. Whereas Rumanian writer Emil Cioran prefers to distance himself from this destabilizing heterogeneity, and, being "incapable of (...) authentic scepticism, and also of humour" (368), chooses to take shelter "in his garret in Paris" (368), Magris does not disavow "the contest between good and evil, truth and falsehood" (368) in everyday life, and endorses the blurring of limits, be it in Bucharest's composite architecture or in the polyvalent and "indistinct substratum of the Rumanian melting-pot" (367) with its "multiple, changing face" (367).

Against the backdrop of the kitsch "superimposition of incompatible elements" (323) of *Art Nouveau* buildings, cultural and ethnic plurality here reinforces the positive value of the adjective "Balkan" that the narrator had previously discussed, defending it from the stereotypical accusation of barbaric and chaotic disorder (341), and replacing these derogatory references with the emphasis on a picturesque variety able to coexist with a sense of order and poise. To be sure, in light of the terrible events of the 1990s, which, after the completion of *Danube*, wiped out the equilibria of part of the Balkans, to find references to the streets of Sarajevo or to its bazaar as confirmations of the positive qualification of the adjective as a synonym for order and efficiency may seem tragically utopian.[14] Arguably, however, this (and certainly not unique) horrible episode of fratricidal violence in the heart of the Old Continent does not weaken Magris's hope that, after the Western European nations' enduring neglect of their central and oriental counterparts, the adjective "other" ("Limes" 71) will finally be dropped in the discourse on Europe.

Therefore, as he reflects on Pannonia, that is, a Hungary still behind the Iron Curtain at the time of the narrator's visit, Magris notices that when "we enter the great Hungarian plains we are certainly entering a Europe that is in part 'other,' a melting-pot composed of elements rather different from those that form the clays of the West" (242), yet he refuses the idea that the border with Austria marks the beginning of an "indistinct (...) Asiatic womb" (242). It is true that the hypothesis of an "Austro-Hungarian solidarity" (245) that the traveler envisions seems feasible only in the gaps between the end of the Hapsburg empire and Soviet totalitarianism. However, even the "ever-provisional equilibrium" (243) that the Hapsburg government meant to keep among its many cultures and sovereignties can inspire current Europe. A poignant example of identitarian and cultural relocation in the Mitteleuropean "ethical-political style" (249) is the possibility of learning to think "with the mind of several peoples" (291) offered by the literary practice of Reiter Robert, a Hungarian poet who, with multiple pseudonyms embodying different ethnic identities, gives voice, in German, to the German minority of the Rumanian Banat region.

Nevertheless, Magris filters this apparently utopian assertion through the critical lens of disenchantment. Attempting once again to avoid unilateral conclusions and definitive conquests, the Danubian traveler further meditates on the Banat as a "mosaic of peoples, a superimposition and stratification of races, powers, jurisdictions" (294), wondering whether that apparent ability to embody and identify with more cultures as in the case of Reiter Robert is actually "a unifying synthesis or a heterogeneous jumble (...) An addition or a subtraction (...) A way to be more abundant or to be Nobody" (292). Magris responds to these musings by positing the need for shareable principles precisely in order to preserve pluralism. If, as he has written more recently in "The Fair of Tolerance,"[15] the protagonist of European culture since its origins is not so much totality as the individual's "irreplaceable uniqueness" ("Fair"), this primacy presupposes "the principle of equal dignity and equal rights" ("Fair") for all individuals, hence "reciprocal tolerance of differences and dialogue between cultures" ("Fair") and value systems even when they are in conflict. At the same time, Europe, according to Magris, has the duty to "renew the awareness and the defence of (…) universal principles" ("Fair"). Magris does not overlook the deeply problematic nature of this contradiction, which interrogates private consciences and public legislations. The growing richness in both diversity and contrasts, and, even more radically, the impossibility to define ourselves univocally, presuppose a cultural and ethical relativism which, however, according to Magris, obliges us to elaborate "a minimum of non-negotiable common values" ("Fair"), and, ultimately, an "inevitable hierarchy" ("Fair"). Because individuals are plural and unstable, they must responsibly agree to "a *quantum* of inalienable ethical universalism" ("Fair").

For Magris, the identity of Europe and the democratic values that Europe is asked to protect require a "continuous and never-ending effort" ("Fair"). In *Danube*, the unresolved tensions between the relative and the universal on the thresholds of old and new Europes remind us that the ideal of Europe as an open community clashes with persisting political and literary localism. The narrator's earlier critique of Heidegger's exclusive conceptualization of the authenticity of homeland and of identity as domestic singularity also applies to the idealization of a closely knit but falsely innocent human network inside the village taken as the center of the universe with which some Rumanian fiction celebrates the "archaic peasant world, the warm cowshed atmosphere of the community" (*Danube* 377). Bauman and Magris address this issue along similar lines. Presenting communitarianism as a predictable reaction to the rapid "liquefaction of modern life" (*Modernity* 170), Bauman alleges that community is often "a cryptonym for the zealously sought yet elusive 'identity'" (171). It justifies its roots and existence by coopting the idealized model of the family homestead to which one belongs by birth, and constructs itself upon an alleged "inner harmony" (172) presupposing a hostile obscure outside. But the "seductive security of *chez soi*" (172) in fact disavows the inner fears and uncertainties which propelled the very search for a communal safe haven, so much so that, Bauman concludes, "[c]ommunal fraternity would be incomplete (…) without that inborn fratricidal inclination" (172). Ultimately, if on the one hand the nation–state affirmed itself by suppressing self-asserting communities and the parochialism of local customs, on the other Bauman remarks that neither nationalism nor patriotism contemplate the possibility of people "belonging together while staying attached to their differences, cherishing and cultivating them" (177). Like the communities it attempts to undermine, nationalism (and patriotism alike) "locks the door, pulls out the door-knockers and disables the doorbells" (177) granting dwelling rights only to those who are inside the velvety shelter and enforcing surveillance and defense at its outer limit.

Magris, too, qualifies both nationalism and municipalism as equally antipatriotic because they are particularistic, hence unable to think and feel big, whereas authentic patriotism can transcend itself (Magris *Storia* 157). The unity that both Bauman and Magris endorse is "achieved daily anew, by confrontation, debate, negotiation and compromise between values, preferences and chosen ways of life and self-identification of many and different, but always self-determining, members of the *polis*" (Bauman *Modernity* 178). *Danube* reinforces this ongoing dialogue with alterity through poignant counterexamples to the glorification of territorial autochtony. For instance, regardless of the widespread "fierce and often aggressive assertion" (212) of one's own identity common to many European national minorities, the Croatians in the Austrian region of Burgenland demand, rather than feel forced, to be assimilated to German culture. Belonging to the culture of their major counterpart is preferable to being recognized uniquely for their smallness. In an intriguing reelaboration of the Heideggerian definition of language as the house of being, the rationale behind this desire for integration is the assumption that "one can change one's language as one changes one's political party or religion" (213) because the world itself is mutable.

Yet with the example of this minority eager to assimilate Magris does not neglect, either, the Slovenian peoples' strong need for redemption from an endemic condition of nation without history, deprived not only of a leading class but even of a recognized identity and language. It is once again with a reference to homes that Magris symbolizes the lack of individual and collective identitarian representation: "Where Are Our Castles?" (221), the title of a section of *Danube*, is borrowed from an essay by the Slovak writer Vladimir Mináč alluding to the contrast between the Hungarian's rich dwellings disseminated on the Slovak territory and the local farmers' poor abodes, the *drevenice*, made of straw and dried manure. For Magris, however, this is an occasion to underscore the complexities of the minority status, which is often coopted as a defensive attitude or as an opportunity to luxuriate in one's own inferiority complex. Courage is required to transcend the rigid categories produced by small and big cultures alike—as Kafka well shows for Magris—so as to attain a balanced and detached vision beyond this ideological polarization.[16] Magris here is in implicit agreement with Deleuze and Guattari, for whom the "minor" condition does not pertain only to marginal literatures but, rather, is the result of a process of deterritorialization that institutes "from within a minor use of even a major language" (Deleuze and Guattari "Minor" 18). Deleuze and Guattari hence maintain that the issue of minority is "the problem of us all" (19), that is, a universal concern in a positive sense, as it demonstrates the potential revolutionary force of all literature. It is on this potential, on the innovative capability of the poetic word, that Magris relies to undermine intolerant, dogmatic thinking.

In this game of reflections and refractions between Europe's past models and future projects, the flowing Danube and the evening wind at an open-air café in a hybrid and eclectic Budapest sound like "the breath of an old Europe" (264) presumably at the margins of the world and only able to consume history. Yet, at the same time, this melancholic hypothetical image of a fading Europe, "a negligible province in a history decided elsewhere" (265) whose spirit seems to be connoted only as a parasite of tradition, leads Magris to contend, nonetheless or *a fortiori*, that Europe "is still there" (265) precisely because we are decreeing its sunset. Just as Budapest should not be viewed as "a setting for the remembrance of past glories" (265) but, rather, as "a robust, full-blooded city" (265), the potential strength of Europe could now be appreciated even more than in the past if Europe could unify "all its multiple energies (...) instead of wearing them away in a perpetual annulment, a state of permanent stalemate" (265). An ice cream in the Hungarian capital hence provides Magris with additional evidence that Europe in Budapest is not just the flavor of antiquity useful for frivolous, nostalgic café conversations but also a living reality in people's minds and a project for the future. To travel—we read in *L'infinito viaggiare*—means to come to terms not only with reality but also with its alternatives and gaps, with history as well as with "other stories that were hampered or suppressed, but not totally erased" (*Infinito* xv), hence still latent in a specific situation. The Danubian narrator's meditations on that apparently mundane occasion is a little epiphany that consolidates his journey in search of Europe as a challenge to nihilism, in a precarious equilibrium between continuity and change.

3.2.4 Flowing home?

If for Hölderlin the Danube is "the journey and the meeting between East and West, the coming-together of the Caucasus and Germany" (278), hence the channel that takes Greece to Europe inverting the flow of the river, the narrator elaborates on this paradoxical conjunction by collapsing the conceptual value of the source and the mouths of the river, the beginning and the end, openness and closure. The traveler's search for freedom against constrictions and repetition leads him to envisage a future that, while on the one hand seems to progressively retreat from the past and the origin, on the other coincides with the potentiality of what still lies ahead. It is through the housing symbolism that the narrator illustrates this dynamics, as he reflects on the individual's "casa natale" (*Danubio* Garzanti 1990: 328), "the house where he was born" (*Danube* 278), awaiting the traveler at the end of his journey. Once again the house is not simply a metaphorical closed space but rather the icon of intimacy coexisting with the uncertainty of life still in progress, which Magris adopts to connote the paradoxical Europeanness represented by the Danube and the geographical and mental spaces it traverses. To conceive and write about Europe, just as about the Danube, is difficult precisely for its "continuous and indistinct" (279) flowing. The provisional quality of the domestic dimension reemerges as ambivalence between the constant protection of a familiar space and the unknown alterity that lies behind (at once in a spatial and temporal sense) when, toward the end of the journey, journey of the river and of his text, the narrator lingers on the "pathos" (*Danubio* Garzanti 1990: 459)[17] of the Danubian border. Underlining the complexity of its nature of bank and bulwark he also reminds us that every frontier, be it territorial or identitarian, "is an imaginary line, beyond which the green is identical to the grass growing on this side" (389). This does not mean to flatten differences in the name of sameness but rather—as Magris also claims in *Utopia e disincanto* (52)—to grasp the intrinsic otherness of the self by debunking the myth of the other side, understanding that everybody is sometimes on this side and other times on the other side. Magris's *Danube* hence operates those inversions and displacements that, in De Certeau's terms, turn the frontier into a crossing and the river into a bridge, an ambiguous construction which, just like a closed door coinciding with "what may be opened" (De Certeau *Practice* 128), "alternatively welds together and opposes insularities. It distinguishes them and threatens them. It liberates from enclosure and destroys autonomy" (128). The spatial and ideological delimitation of the frontier is itself "the bridge that opens the inside to its other" (129). It paradoxically trangresses the limit by revealing the latent alterity contained in the interior the moment it objectifies it outside.

The very delta of Magris's river is an "endless flowing" (*Danube* 467) embodying De Certeau's "logic of ambiguity" (*Practice* 128). Like its origin, its end is vague, plural, multiple, scattered. Even the arbitrary decision to choose Sulina as the official point where the waters of the Danube are straightforwardly channeled toward the sea does not suffice to isolate "the hypothetical point of dissolving" (*Danube* 398) from the "mixture of transition" (398) and trespass. The "domesticated Danube" (397) throws itself into the great sea challenging limits and rules in order to abandon itself "to all the waters and oceans of the entire globe" (401). Its uncountable branches go their own way at their own pace; "si emancipano dall'imperiosa unità-identità" (*Danubio* 467) [they emancipate from the imperious unity-identity].[18]

Yet the conceptual point of arrival for the river and for subjectivity is not total disappearance. This would decree that Magris's itinerant character has arrived at port, home, whereas in fact the journey into rooted homelessness goes on, through life and other literary domestic spaces. If the global flow at the Danube's mouth seems to dilute the local and European dimension that the entire path of the river had traced, Magris's *Microcosms* and *Blindly* adopt the topos of housing to develop additional aesthetic and ethical implications of the experience of belonging to a transitory domestic space. Whereas *Microcosms* further elaborates on the role of borders in enclosing and defining temporary dwellings, *Blindly* stages the tragic loss of home and homeland to plunge us into a destabilizing globality that reinstates with a vengeance the vital need for an abode as the space of the human and of *humanitas* in the very act of mourning for its destruction.

Notes

1 See, for instance, Magris's 1966 preface to *Il mito absburgico* (7) and *La vita non è innocente* 38.
2 For a synthetic overview of the many nuances of and controversies about the different terms associated with this complex area, see Cornis Pope and Neubauer *History* 1–7.
3 On this aspect, see also Daria Trentini "Idea di Mitteleuropa" 543.
4 Magris underlines that, in this hegemonic design of German culture as leader of Central Europe, on the one hand Germany seems to have the potential to act as a sort of "Esperanto of Mitteleuropa" ("Mitteleuropa" 146), able to generate cohesiveness among different ethnicities and cultures, yet, on the other hand, the catastrophic epilogue of its history mercilessly destroys its own internal component which authenticated its "unifying and

supranational factor *par excellence*" (146), namely, "the Jewish-Germany symbiosis" (146). This is all the more tragic because, as Magris highlights also in *Lontano da dove*, it is precisely Jewish culture that, in addition to, and even more than German culture, can define itself as a "supranational, unifying element and nexus" (146).

5   As Magris reminds us in *L'infinito viaggiare*, despite the ultimate failure of the Mitteleuropean project, the need remains of a unity of civilizations respectful of all diversities. The new political scenarios that have emerged from the upheavals in the former Habsburg empire, and, more extensively, the new Europe he envisions must not be an archipelago of aggressive nations and ethnic groups obsessed by their own particularity (*Infinito* 173).

6   See Marchand's comments in "Lire Claudio Magris." Magris himself emphasizes the enduring fecundity of the Mitteleuropean historic-cultural legacy by defining it as "a precious silt, an underground sap that effectively flows into the construction of the new Europe" (Magris and Ciccarelli 405).

7   The English translation "literature as moving house" (*Danube* 18) is less effective.

8   Missing the echo of Magris's previous work, the English translator of *Danubio* has rendered "illazione" with the less satisfactory term "deduction" (*Danube* 28).

9   In this opposition between the two rivers symbolizing their respective cultures, Magris condenses the substantial difference he lays out in his article on Mitteleuropa between the plural Danubian civilization, aware of the precariousness of individual identity and wary of grand syntheses and of universality, on the one hand, and, on the other, German culture "which created the great totalizing systems" ("Mitteleuropa" 149).

10 The Italian original for this expression, namely, "un'arida epifania, un'inutilità che stringe il cuore" (*Danubio* Garzanti 198), expresses more strongly this loss of feelings caused by the aseptic architecture of Wittgenstein's home.

11 For a discussion of the border as barrier and bridge in Magris's works see also Ciccarelli "Crossing Borders" 344–345.

12 This is also what emerges from Magris's short monologue *Essere già stati* (*To Have Been*), where the idea of "having been," that is, the attachment to one's own personal past as opposed to a spontaneous embrace of the openness of the present and future is associated with certain features of a typically Central European homeliness that Magris attempts to temper in his own poetics. Here the "stagnant Pannonian air" (*To Have Been* 11) connotes Central Europe as an "uncertain and accommodating space where everything is as light as a feather" (11). Central Europe is condensed in the image of the grandmother's protective house, without "sharp corners" (13) or ambushes or other dangers. In this cozy domestic environment, life is

"secure, safe from any accident" (13) but "nothing more can happen" (14) because [e]verything has already happened" (14).

13 For a discussion of the stereotypical Eastern Europe different from its Western counterpart in *Danube* see Czorycki "Figures."

14 Magris himself rethinks the political and poetic message of *Danube* in light of more recent historical events in Europe in his article "Danubio e post-Danubio."

15 Originally delivered as a speech in The Hague in 2001 on the occasion of the Erasmus Prize and republished in Italian as "Le frontiere del dialogo" in *La storia non è finita*.

16 In support of this need for openness and freedom to reappropriate one's own history without essentializing experiences or sacrificing one's own relationship with the rest of the world, we can consider the unusual perspective on the relationship between Europe and Ottoman civilization offered by a Viennese exhibition that captures the Danubian narrator's attention for its unconventional interpretation of the dynamics of intercultural contacts. Rather than an opposition between winners and losers or civilization and barbarism, the exhibition highlights the ephemerality of each victory or defeat that inevitably occurs to any people. The European past hence appears to the Western visitor as "a history unified in its fragments, (...) composed of crescents as well as crosses, of Capuchin cords and of turbans" (*Danube* 177), and reveals that every history and every identity consists of difformity and pluralities, of cultural and ethnic exchanges and subtractions "which make each nation and individual the child of a regiment" (178).

17 Despite its importance in Magris's overall poetics, the term "pathos" in the original Italian text has disappeared from the English translation, which renders it as "the frontier reeks of insecurity" (*Danube* 389).

18 Although this phrase represents a significant connection between the geographical and the philosophical levels in Magris's reflection, it is missing in the English translation of *Danube*.

4
From Snug Refuges to Ghastly Cells

Abstract: *Starting from a comparative analysis of Walter Benjamin and Magris's technique of microcosmic representation of physical and mental spaces, the chapter shows how, like Benjamin's* flâneur, *the narrator of* Microcosms *walks through circumscribed sites that constitute small households of memories relevant to Magris's personal life and cultural formation. While preserving their autonomy, these places become* loci *of constant transition that expand in the narrative, evoking simultaneously the necessity and the vanity of borders. However, Magris's more recent novel* Blindly *also highlights the risk of fetishizing these geographic and emotional temporal dwelling places. In a global identitarian and cultural Babel, the protagonist's ghastly journey through jails, prison-islands, torturing chambers, and makeshift hiding places exposes the devastating side of precariousness and marginalization, indicting Europe's lack of responsibility.*

Keywords: *Alla cieca* [*Blindly*]; café; globalization; memory; *Microcosmi* [*Microcosms*]; Walter Benjamin

Pireddu, Nicoletta. *The Works of Claudio Magris: Temporary Homes, Mobile Identities, European Borders*. New York: Palgrave Macmillan, 2015. DOI: 10.1057/9781137488046.0007.

4.1 *Microcosms*: the *flâneur* in his homescapes

> Every journey is above all a return, even if the return, almost always, lasts very little and it's soon time to leave. (Magris *Microcosms* 31)

Written in 1997 and awarded the "Premio Strega," *Microcosms* can be considered the most autobiographical of Magris's fictional works, even if the narrator uses the first-person pronoun very rarely throughout the book. It depicts, as Magris explains, the discovery of increasingly tiny and limited places, which, however, have nothing to do with either an indifferent minimalism or the hostile particularism of regressive small homelands (*Fra il Danubio e il mare* 31). Many of the characters and stories that interwine in these little worlds belong to the author's own interior landscape but they merge with other real or symbolic voices and spaces, all working at once as "provisional stops and faithful dwellings" (31) in the individual's earthly transit.

Like all borders, the geographical and conceptual frontiers of Europe are for Magris at once "precarious and unavoidable" (*Microcosms* 74), and just as *Danube* does with the Mitteleuropean river, *Microcosms* evokes simultaneously their necessity and their vanity through other apparently limited and circumscribed places relevant to Magris's life and cultural formation, like Trieste's Caffè San Marco, the public garden, the city itself, or the forest of Mount Nevoso—households of Magris's own memory which, while preserving their autonomy, also expand in the narrative, overlapping and merging with more extended sites, just as locality and globalism intersect in *Danube*'s dynamic concept of Europeanness.

4.1.1 Image masonry

With his depiction of personal spaces as steps in the itinerary of a multicentric subjective consciousness that renders objects of representation indistinguishable from their interpretation, the author of *Microcosms* adopts a technique that recalls Walter Benjamin's treatment of the homology between city and self as sites of memory and experience in which private and public coalesce. This connection with the German philosopher and cultural theorist, so far overlooked by criticism, can throw further light upon Magris's oblique narrative self-portrait as well as upon the implications for the role of the domestic space in his poetics.

The very title of Magris's work evokes an idea that informs Benjamin's approach to representation. As we can see in "The Image of Proust" and in "A Berlin Chronicle," Benjamin adopts the term "microcosm" (*Illuminations* 215; *One Way* 296) to define the blend of real and imaginary spaces in his critical explorations. His impressionistic renditions of urban landscapes, which he labeled "thought-images" (*Denkbilder*), are precisely miniature scenes that crystallize fleeting ordinary events. With a technique that also informs Magris's work, Benjamin captures subjective everyday experiences in flux, and, through free association, merging concrete details and imagination, turns them into objective criticism. From Theodor Adorno to Susan Sontag, most critics have indeed emphasized the "microscopic gaze"[1] as a key element in Benjamin's analytical perspective. In a game of mirrors between micro- and macrocosms, Benjamin treats his object of investigation at once as a fragment and as a world without depriving it of its singularity, and engages with it intellectually and emotionally.

Benjamin's *Denkbild* of Naples in *One Way Street*, for instance, not only transfers the porosity of Neapolitan stones to the urban architecture but also uses it to visualize the correspondence between the city's configuration and its inhabitants' way of life. "Porosity is the inexhaustible law of the life of this city, reappearing everywhere" (*One Way* 171). Just as "[b]uilding and action interpenetrate in the courtyard, arcades, and stairways" (169), so Neapolitan private life is equally "dispersed, porous, and commingled" (174). Hence "[p]orosity results not only from the indolence of the Southern artisan, but also, above all, from the passion for improvisation, which demands that space and opportunity be at any time preserved" (170). Similarly, gazing at oyster stalls in Marseille or boarding a streetcar in Moscow, Benjamin connects a series of self-contained, fragmentary impressions about life in the French and Russian towns that turn into sensuous experiences for both the visitor and the reader,[2] and generate lyric commentaries on the subject and the material environment foregrounding a physical and emotional proximity between the urban space, the individual's own recollections and collective historical memory. The cityscape as a private and simultaneously public connection between self and space, past and present, persists in Benjamin's seminal works on Berlin and Paris. Benjamin's representation of the French capital, for instance, embraces both the author's personal view in the present and the cultural and literary legacy of the place as it reconstructs the phantasmagoria of nineteenth-century Parisian streets through the double filter of the *flâneur* figure in Baudelaire's poems. Through the *flâneur*'s gaze, Benjamin experiences Paris like Baudelaire's alienated man, the city-dweller of the arcades, "which are house no less than street" (*Selected* III, 40), "on the threshold—of the metropolis and of the middle class" (39), at the crossroads where "the intelligentsia sets foot in the marketplace" (40), not owned by either, and not at home in either.[3]

The adoption of the term "microcosm" by both Benjamin and Magris hence substantiates significant common features in their respective approaches to physical and mental spaces, both based upon the conception of the writer as a participant–observer. Benjamin maintains that in the small worlds of his investigations "no knowledge is possible without the self-knowledge of what is to be known, and that this can be called into wakefulness by one center of reflection (the observer) in another (the thing) only insofar as the first, through repeated reflections, intensifies itself to the point of encompassing the second" ("Criticism" *Selected* I, 147). Similarly, as Magris writes about his technique in *Microcosms*, despite the apparent concealment of the narrative "I," it is as though one detected its traces in the sand and, by looking around, seeing the surrounding landscape and people, and listening to the stories that occurred in those places, one attempted to understand who actually passed through them, what this person felt, what meaning and destiny his/her life had (*Fra il Danubio* 32). Just as in Benjamin's conceptualization of memory "the human figures recede before the place itself" (*Selected Writings* 2, 609), writing for Magris implies disappearing into impersonality, yet simultaneously wandering in search of subjectivity. Remarking Benjamin's attraction for small things, Susan Sontag underlines that "[t]o miniaturize is to make portable" ("Introduction" *One Way* 19), which is "the ideal form of possessing things for a wanderer, or a refugee" (19). As both writers wander in their microcosms, at once "a whole (...) and a fragment" (19), they merge self and city in narratives combining commentary, memory, description, fiction, biography, autobiography in an always incomplete, labyrinthine topography.

A major *Denkbild* in the geographical, mental, and affective landscapes of *Microcosms*, the topos of dwelling in Magris's book can be connoted with the words that Benjamin adopts for the function of the house in Naples: it is "far less the refuge into which people retreat than the inexhaustible reservoir from which they flood out" (*One Way* 174). Just as for Benjamin the city shapes the dweller's experience, memory, and subjectivity as he moves through the cityscape, the thought-image of domesticity in Magris's own *flâneur* renders the spaces of *Microcosms* at once private interiors and public urban sites. Yet the movement within the material world deprives the subject of its own integrity as much as it maps and expands its identity. To walk, according to De Certeau, is "to lack a place. It is the indefinite process of being absent and in search of a proper" (*Practice* 102). The urban environment is "only a pullulation of passer-by, a network of residences temporarily appropriated (…), a shuffling among pretenses of the proper, a universe of rented spaces haunted by a nowhere or by dreamed-of places" (103). Indeed, evanescent scenes and impressions, discontinuous itineraries, fusion of past and present, individual and collective memories, real and literary references seem to align the spatial experience of Benjamin and Magris's mobile subjects to a condition of self-dispossession. This constant juxtaposition of settings, however, does not entail nostalgia for a stable abode, a monolithic individual identity and a consistent personal history, nor does it lead to complete disintegration. Just as Benjamin does not push his cityscapes to the hallucinatory extremes of Surrealists, despite being influenced by them, Magris does not aim at the destabilizing, chaotic fragmentation that characterizes, for instance, Arjun Appadurai's notion of "scapes" in *Modernity at Large*, namely, constantly shifting settings within which intricate globalizing processes deconstruct space, culture, and identity. Magris's subject, too, resists hegemonic approaches, but feels at home in the dialectical tension between dis-membering and re-membering.

4.1.2 Domestic aromas

Among the many microcosms of non-alienating precariousness working as a surrogate of the house, the café very frequently appears in Magris as a comforting place of rest from which to contemplate, from afar, from behind the glass, the "convulsive gleam" (*Atlante* 59) of life. Once again, the Benjaminian space offers intimations of this transient domesticity blending home and city. A coffeehouse regular himself in his Parisian years, Benjamin in his "A Berlin Chronicle" lingers on the youthful time "when the Berlin cafés played a part in [their] lives" (*One Way* 309). Even though back then he had not yet developed a "daily need" (310) for frequenting coffeehouses and his first café "was more a strategic quarter than a place of siesta" (310), he also ascribes an increasing sense of coziness to the coffeehouse as he acknowledges his "much more intimate terms" (311) with the "snug recesses" (312) of the Princess Café, which they were "in the habit of patronizing as occupants of private boxes" (312), aiming to be "enclosed in an environment that isolated [them]" (312). The central role of the café in urban life is evident in the multiple reasons that Benjamin gives for its popularity across different social strata, an attention that even prompts him to imagine a veritable "Physiology of Coffeehouses" (311), starting from the distinction between "professional and recreational establishments" (311).

Already in *Il mito absburgico* Magris defines the café as the "*locus amoenus*" (*Mito* 206) of Mitteleuropean literature, a symbol of *humanitas*, of the serene intimacy and respectful distinction exuding from that bygone epoch. In *Danube*, that locus offers the Mitteleuropean traveler the relief of a house outside one's home, and, with its combination of habitual activities and unforeseen movements and events, extends the ritual and affective value of the café experience to urban life as whole, connoting the city itself "as one vast café" (*Danube* 215). In *Microcosms* it is, in particular, the Triestine Caffè San Marco that functions as "a sort of hospice (...), a temporary refuge" (*Microcosms* 13) for those in need of warmth and snugness, and at the same time as the embodiment of life itself as a sea port, hosting a plurality of voices and of social roles, and hence the negation of any suffocating endogamy (7). Additional references to a domestic setting intensify his idea of protected openness: fear may knock at the door, but, if it is faith that opens, it dissipates all danger threats as it withstands the anxiety of the unknown. Yet Magris also laments the dearth of incentives to host the unfamiliar, the tendency to "close doors, (...) to bolt everything, even the windows, without realizing that this way there's no air and (...) eventually all you hear is the sound of your own headache" (10). The welcoming ambiance of the café teaches precisely to overcome the fear of a challenging new, so as to let in the uncertain, the foreign, the unusual, the precarious, abandoning our attachment to completeness and self-referentiality. It is for this reason that the café—a site of impermanence, where one sits as on a journey in a hotel, a train, or on the road—is also "a place for writing" (*Microcosms* 10), where the pen penetrates with perplexity and obstinacy into the world's "cavity of uncertainty" (12).

This fertile connection between the coffeehouse and creative activity renders Magris a paramount contemporary dweller of what has been recently defined as "the thinking space" (Haine *Thinking* 1–22), that is, the café as an institutional locus of intellectual and artistic productivity nourished by multiple influences and debates, which gave birth to the most relevant aesthetic and philosophical movements throughout European modernity. The literary and cultural history of Italy, in particular, has been defined by iconic sites like the Venitian Caffè Florian, a reference point for artists and intellectuals across centuries, from Goldoni and Casanova to Wagner and

D'Annunzio, the Caffè delle Giubbe Rosse in Florence, the alcove of Italian poetic hermeticism and of militant and avant-garde literary journals like *La Voce* and *Solaria*, or the Caffè Greco in Rome, with its numerous illustrious habitués among whom Stendhal, Schopenhauer, and Carlo Levi. It is generally assumed that the café as a productive site of liberal thinking lost relevance after the Second World War. Yet Claudio Magris offers an intriguing counter-example to this cultural shift, given the significance of this place to his personal experience and literary activity[4] precisely for its inspiring blend of "social interaction and solitary introspection" (Haine *Thinking* 3).

"All, at their respective tables, are close to and distant from the person next to them" (*Microcosms* 11), Magris writes of the café ambiance, highlighting a paradoxical condition of homeliness which, precisely by preventing absolutist views, acts as a guarantee of measure and openness. Its "familiar anonymity"(12) allows one to get rid of one's ego "as if it were a shell" (12) and to be influenced by a plurality of adjacent realities. Therefore the coffeehouse for Magris is a microcosm of a world which is itself the habitat of a precarious but exciting multiplicity. The narrator summarizes the experience in the café as a pleasant sequence of carefree actions—"To write, to take a break, chat, play at cards" (12)—as time flows, untroubled. The kaleidoscope of disparate daily events and past recollections that the narrator evokes renders the Caffè San Marco a protagonist of Trieste's history but also indicates a way of escaping the tyranny of self-centeredness and ideological parochialism. Indeed, "[a]t these tables it is not possible to found a school, draw up ranks, mobilize followers and emulators, recruit disciples" (11). The authenticity of the Caffè San Marco for Magris lies precisely in the blend of "conservative loyalty and (…)liberal pluralism" (7) of its regular customers, which he condenses in the image of the café as "a buzz of voices, a disconnected and uniform choir" (8). By contrast, with the term "pseudocafés" (7) he categorizes all those sites of intellectual discourses—be they coffeehouses, educational and cultural institutions, political circles, or exclusive clubs—which, by hosting a single tribe, negate life as the triumph of variety. By defining the café as a "place of disenchantment" (11), Magris ascribes to the experience of this variety that lucid cautiousness which, in line with what he spells out in *Utopia e disincanto*, allows one to identify false masters and ignore their misleading promises of redemption.

The owners of Caffè San Marco are "like the founders of shelters for the homeless" (13), who hence reinforce the function of the coffeehouse itself as a provisional safe haven. The "tavola" (*Microcosmi* 14) at the Caffè San Marco (at once the table at the coffeehouse and a wooden board in a metaphorical stormy sea) offers the shipwrecked a handhold to which to cling. Once again, however, this chain of figurative associations does not delineate an openness without boundaries but, rather, a protective domestic dimension that coexists with the need for movement and freedom. Indeed, the soft blanket of smoke in the coffeehouse is transfigured into a "cocoon in which the chrysalis would like to shut itself up indefinitely" (6) to avoid its painful metamorphosis into a butterfly. Yet the pen of the writer settled in the café "bursts the cocoon and frees the butterfly" (6). Through the café ambiance, however, Magris subjects the power of writing itself to the limits set by a moderate and critical attitude. Surrounded by the indifference of other café-goers and the scornful expressions of the masks on the walls, "the pen is dipped, willingly or otherwise, into ink diluted with humility and irony" (10). If the writer is often in the grip of a "latent delirium of omnipotence" (10) and dares to pronounce grand univocal truths about life and death, the coffeehouse, as a sort of metonymy for Trieste, tempers the alleged power of self-sufficiency. No customer, not even the writer, can leave his/her conceited personal imprint because we are all "nobody" (12).

Writing is, itself, "a shipwreck" (10) and "salvation" (10), and the pen "a lance that wounds and heals; it pierces the floating wood and leaves it to the mercy of the waves, but it also plugs the wood" (10). Like "Noah's Ark" (3), the café saves the writers, together with all the other customers at the mercy of the deluge of life, offering everybody a provisional shelter, without priorities or exclusions. Elaborating on this image in "The Self That Writes," Magris defines the Caffè San Marco in particular as "the Noah's Ark of Central Europe" ("Self" 20), extending this characterization to other significant coffeehouses beyond his native town and home country, be it the cafés of Turin, the city where Magris spent over a decade as a university student and subsequently as a professor of German literature, the Caffè Central in Vienna appearing in many of his literary works, or those in numerous other European cities where he regularly sojourns. He thus further enriches this poignant instance of mobile, temporary dwelling by rendering it the embodiment of the Mitteleuropean tolerant, conciliatory pluralism.

Jürgen Habermas stresses the social interaction and the discursive, ultimately political, involvement that the institution of the café promotes by bringing together "the sphere of private people" (*Structural* 27) into what he defines as "the public sphere" (27–29; 33). Elaborating along similar lines, sociologist Ray Oldenburg presents the café as a "third place" (Oldenburg *Good* 21–22), which hosts practices and relations distinct from the increasingly private dimension of the "first place" represented by home life, as well as from the purposeful and productive activity at the workplace, or, for Oldenburg, the "second place." Within this triad, the peculiarity of the café for Oldenburg lies in its ability to facilitate informal community building in the public sphere thanks to its welcoming, inclusive, democratic atmosphere. For his part, Magris occupies a highly significant place in the discourse on café and intellectual life, because he foregrounds the complex function of the coffeehouse, portraying it not simply as an unconditional promoter of writing and of cultural exchange but also as a place that problematizes those practices. Reelaborating a claim by Modernist Austrian writer Hermann Bahr, who equated the café to a Platonic academy, Magris in *Microcosms* points out that in this academy there is room for chatting and storytelling but not for teaching and preaching. The only things that can be learned are sociability and disenchantment (11). His critical engagement with the café as a site of intellectual dialogue lingers on the tension between proximity and distance in that social context, not only because in order for the coffeehouse to stimulate creativity it needs a balance between conviviality and detachment, but, above all, because with the topos of the temporary home Magris blurs the line between the privacy of an enclosed, stable domestic space and the open, transient communal experience at the café.

Furthermore, from the homely yet public sphere of the café in Magris's works we can draw, in particular, the author's European consciousness. The coexistence of pluralism with respect for the other that Magris underscores in the social interaction at the tables of the Caffè San Marco epitomizes the feature that in intellectuals like Denis de Rougemont and George Steiner renders the café a veritable icon of Europeanness. For De Rougemont, the café is an unavoidable element in the typical European square, and, together with the press, the expression of the intrinsically European meaning of democracy, founded upon "freedom of discussion, free party activity and freedom for the opposition which may tomorrow be the majority" (Rougemont *Meaning* 44). Likewise, in his discussion of the cultural notion of Europe, Steiner claims that "Europe is made up of coffee houses" (*Idea of Europe* 17) and that "[s]o long as there are coffee houses, the 'idea of Europe' will have content" (18). This is due precisely to the café's open yet defined boundaries surrounding a "humanized" (19) space that functions as "the club of the spirit and the *poste-restante* of the homeless" (18), and that hosts both discursive connections and oppositions, as in an "*agora*, the locus of eloquence and rivalry" (18). From a similar perspective, Magris often avows that the café is his home away from home, and ascribes this sense of domesticity to European unity, which he considers "an extension of the dialogue and the feeling of belonging together ("Fair"). From the café to Trieste and to Mitteleuropa at large, the concentric worlds of Magris's *Microcosms* shade off into one another and hence materialize the very idea of Europe and Europeanness as an "effimero trascolorare" (*Microcosmi* 44),[5] a fleeting chromatic mutability of different identities and cultures, like the "changing colors of life" (*Microcosms* 39) evoked in the chapter "Valcellina" or the lake's mutable spectrum of hues at Anterselva in "Antholz": "the green on the trees is black, white becomes gold, a bronze gold that gets darker and is suddenly blue" (231). Its edges—"confini" (*Microcosmi* 227) in Italian—are sharp but "quick to dissolve" (*Microcosms* 231).

Just as Magris's "tumultuous and cross-bred" (234) Trieste is the exemplary embodiment of a big café, its public garden is a threshold and a microcosm of the world. As the narrator and the reader traverse it, passing through the book's "forests, lagoons, cities, mountains, snows, seas" (268), it clearly appears that "it was all there already, from the beginning" (268). In the eponymous chapter, "Public Garden," the borders traced by vegetation or born of children's games seem to compartmentalize the "multiform spaces" (236) of the garden in "limited perimeters" (236). Yet the stream that gushes from the past of those places, evoked by historical reminiscences linked to the statue of Italian botanist and politician Muzio de' Tommasini, challenges the rigor of borders both when it connects a Slovenian neighborhood with Italian patriotism, and when its waters turn red with the deadly violence that lacerates intercultural relationships because "in that muddy water it is impossible to tell blood from blood" (244). Trieste, "the frontier city" (244) by definition—like the town of Grado, another "border, a strip marking several frontiers" (72)—hence shows not only its optimistic face as a melting pot of different ethnicities, languages, and cultures, but also the more dramatic one, that of a land further torn by frontiers that transform its natural multiplicity into the horror of violent fragmentation.

Trieste, we are reminded, is "everything and its opposite" (250). This ambivalent and hybrid nature is that of life itself, with its "contiguity of the seedy and the sublime" (250) effectively synthesized by another eminent dweller in the microcosm of Magris's garden, James Joyce. Magris portrays this famous adoptive Triestine citizen as the heir of a centuries-old cult of "the sacredness of (...) the home and the family" (250), associating him with a homecoming and with an identitarian self-sameness that the subject, however, regains only by passing through an inevitable dislocation and relocation staged by verbal transgression. This, we can argue, is yet another sign of that vital "Triesteness" (251) that embodies a "European dimension" (251) fighting against "fossilized culture" (251) as much as against "the chtonic powers" (241) of wilderness. The microcosm of the Triestine public garden hence substantiates the homology between culture and cultivation through which, like gardening, Europeanness can be conceived as "the art of harmonizing" (241) and of establishing the "*civitas*" (248) of a collective cultural legacy over the dark indistinction of real and metaphorical forests.

4.1.3 Residential antinomies

In *Microcosms* this idea of Europe as measured opening, neither diluted in indistinction nor anchored to the forced stability of self-identity, clashes with another kind of borderline place, another uninterrupted frontier "dividing and uniting" (197), that of municipal nationalisms. Although they can be crossed unawarely, these liminal areas are a material reminder of that alarming Europe of particularisms already denounced in *Danube*—a perversion of the very notion of microcosm that shapes Magris's book, and, as we will see in the next section, a foreshadowing of the tragedy of history in his subsequent novel *Blindly*. For instance, according to the narrator in the chapter "Antholz," being in the Austro-Italian borderline region of Tyrol is not tantamount to being in a world of provisional homes, difference and change, but, rather, to dwelling in the "Land," made of boroughs that replace the nation with ethnicity and the state with the region. An exclusive "us" barricades itself behind the doors of a "cult of diversities that are no longer loved as so many concrete expressions of human universality, but rather (…) idolized now as absolute values, each one rabidly at odds with the rest" (206–207). Magris dismantles this dangerous unilateral attitude by showing that, if the Brenner represents the geographic and historical dividing line between "life's two opposing and complementary scenarios" (197), namely, the Adriatic sea and continental Mitteleuropa, in fact travelers cross this border without even realizing it. This easy, imperceptible passage against all cartographic and ideological odds has a paramount symbolic value. It confirms Magris's conviction that any kind of purity, including the ethnic one, corresponds to "a subtraction" (205) culminating with a zero in the most rigorous cases.

Against the backdrop of the extremist cult of "the uncontaminated *Heimat* among the mountains" (195), in "Antholz" Magris illustrates an alternative view of home, through snapshots of local life in the eponymous South Tyrolean valley where the inhabitants' customs and rituals offer occasions to develop intercultural relations. The everyday work and family activities of characters like Beppino and Jakob intertwine with those of the narrator's own family members, who are their guests at each visit to the area, and share meals and pleasurable moments all together. The narrator's home becomes the ultimate repository of the household's memories of Antholz thanks to their tangible mementos. Each of their trips to the valley ends with the purchase a piece of a porcelain dish set which, in addition to serving as "calendar and reckoning of the years" (209), preserves a symbolic and affective attachment between their acquaintances' warm hospitality in Antholz and their own family meals in the company of other guests. The emotional continuity between Antholz and the protagonist's household is further enhanced by other local places that function as substitutes for their own domestic hearth or that indirectly reinforce the sense of community. For instance, the *Stube* of the Herberhof Hotel, like the Caffè San Marco, constitutes a temporary abode for the narrator's writing activity, whereas the Weger–Keller building foregrounds the value of collectivity against "the vain little ego" (222) with its Baroque frescoes representing "the humility and the glory of a common destiny—being born, living and dying" (222). This image prompts the narrator to underline the binding effect of transience as he presents death in terms of "a rite of social cohesion, a centripetal force" (223).

However, just as the disrupting forces of savagery in Magris's Triestine public garden are always ready to attack the domesticating power of *cultura* [culture] and *coltura* [cultivation], *Microcosms* offsets the symbolism of the house as hospitality, sharing, and openness, with its negative double, a hallmark of Magris's dialectical literary world. The bunkers that Mussolini built on the mountain at the frontier with its German ally are a reminder of the manipulations that the borderline Alto Adige region had to undergo in the strife between the Fascist and the Nazi regimes, and of the ultimate break-up of the "unity of their own land and stock" (203) in South Tyrol's troubled assimilation to either Italian land or German national culture. Niederrasen is "a hybrid town" (204), and the borders of the valley intersect like the ski tracks on the snow because history has further divided this already tiny "geopolitical atom (…) into an erratic fractal multiplicity, into the tortuous plurality of all feudal macro- or microcosms" (205).

Current Europe is thus expected to mediate between "the arrogance of the majority" (245) and "the resentment of the minority" (245), and literature has a specific responsibility in this dialogue. Resuming the discussion he started in *Danube* on literary expressions of marginality, Magris in

Microcosms questions the "polemical obsession with the border" (228) in the rhetoric of frontier writing, whenever authors tend to appropriate it as their own exclusive prerogative, and almost with a sort of self-complacency for their minority status. "Südtirolese writers should be a bit—just a bit—less Südtirolese or rather less anti-Südtirolese and forget their umbilical cords" (229). Magris here highlights how identitarian ambivalence can be exploited with bad faith whenever an alleged lack of representation and of participation in European life is coopted strategically to gain visibility on the European scene. As he observes in *Utopia e disincanto*, the complacent declaration of extraneousness to any precise identity, which often prompts frontier literature to flaunt its own non-belonging, can become a convenient alibi and a stale repertoire of clichés (*Utopia* 60). In response to this tendentious attitude aimed at preserving a false peculiarity, *Microcosms* envisages the possibility of a Europe in which home and homeland are delimited by geographical and conceptually provisional borders, like those of the forest of Mount Nevoso. In the chapter devoted to this karst plateau in the Slovenian Alps, the narrator of *Microcosms* meditates on its uncertain extension, realizing, however, that although its gates are invisible thresholds, "one clearly feels them as they open and they close, and when one is inside or outside" (*Microcosms* 99). If it is true that the arrival of history in those secluded places is documented by chronicles that talk "with obsessive insistence" (106) about frontiers and borders, Magris condemns this defensive and unilateral attitude emphasizing that "the woods are at once the glorification and the nullification of borders: a plurality of differing, opposing worlds, though still within the great unity that embraces and dissolves them" (107).

Likewise, in the chapter "Lagoons," devoted to the coastal landscape in the Friulian city of Grado, the agent of dissolution of a unified, solid and permanent habitat and self is liquidity, which, with an additional step with respect to *Danube*, here exhibits its contradictory nature. Water is at once "life and a threat to life; it erodes, submerges, fertilizes, bathes, abolishes" (57). Simultaneously transparent and sludgy, the lagoon washes away "the usual distinctions between clean and dirty" (56). The ambivalence of this liquid environment hence also becomes a metaphor that substantiates Magris's ethico-political vision. Indeed, the "precarious and unavoidable" (74) dividing line between the lagoon and the sea is here presented as the epitome of Magris's conception of any border, and leads the narrator to linger on the complex geopolitical vicissitudes of the borderline Grado area, itself "a strip marking several frontiers. Between land and sea, (...) open sea and closed lagoon,

(...) mainland and maritime civilization" (72), and ultimately between "the airy marine ethos of Venice [and] a continental and problematic *Mitteleuropa*" (73). On many occasions across centuries, the contested boundaries of the lagoon have turned into a fatal front line that claimed massive sacrifice of human lives, from the bloody devastation of Grado by its rival city of Aquileia back in 1023 to the carnage of the First World War. A way of neutralizing the lethal power of borders, Magris suggests, is hence "to consider oneself and to put oneself on the other side" (73), incorporating alterity as constitutive parts of our own being. Otherness and ephemerality are inscribed in the islands that appear and disappear with the tide. This protean landscape lends itself to a "slow, aimless wandering" (54) in search of "signs of metamorphosis" (54) because its gradual mutation coexists with a "tenacious resistance of form to extinction" (54). Movement and changes are visible and tangible, and invite the traveler to linger on a rotten trunk not totally consumed, a crumbling dune or the "traces of lives lived in an old house" (54), as in the case of the remains of the "*casoni*" (56), the typical building of the lagoon islands. The *casoni* epitomize the precariousness of the abode. Used both as dwellings and as storehouses for fishing, and made of poor materials like wood, canes, and mud, the *casoni* effectively represent the kind of shelter that for Tuan requires almost constant construction and repair because they combine "persistence of form with ephemerality of substance" (Tuan *Space* 104).

The narrator-*flâneur*'s journey through what I would call the homescapes of *Microcosms* synthesizes the mobility and transience in Magris's conceptualization of the self and of the domestic space through the various sites he visits. If the decisive step of a voyage "is the one that brings the foot back onto land or back home" (88), the restaurant that the narrator has elected as his ritual stopover before his return to Trieste "is almost home and has been so for many years" (88), yet this "almost" contains precisely the temporary quality of the dwelling place that defines the subject and his world. Like the coffeehouse in Magris's writings, an authentic inn is "a seaport" (89) much appreciated by travelers whenever they wish to stop and rest for a while. Similarly, in the chapter "Apsyrtides" memories themselves become a "felice dimora" (*Microcosmi* Garzanti 1999: 153), a happy abode[6] where past and present, events experienced on the isle of Cherso and their narratives, merge in an ambiance of "reflective familiarity" (155) like that of the "white houses on the shore" (155).

The church, too, is a temporary home, and the ultimate shelter in the book. In "Lagoon" it is weakened, like the *casoni*, by the action of natural elements. "Besieged (...) by water, [it] is both a hard-pressed vessel calling for assistance and a dam or ark that offers help to those who are in peril of drowning" (58). Almost a memento of human transience, it shares its precariousness with the inn, two liberal places where visitors are not asked "from and under which flag or insignia they travel" (60). Magris brings them together precisely for their common openness "to travellers passing by and looking to rest for a moment" (60).[7] Not accidentally, after coffeehouses and inns, it is in the temporary shelter of the church that the itinerant protagonist of *Microcosms* completes his meandering journey, a conclusion that, however, does not mark a definitive closure. In the last chapter, "The Vault," the idea of the end seems to allude to a wider scheme, in this case an eschatological one, which implies the crossing of a more crucial border than all spatial boundaries, namely, that of life itself, but with the hope of waking up on the other side. Father Guido offers the protagonist the chance to rest in the church for a while and, in the dim light, the niche of the baptismal font reminds him of a hollow tree trunk where "you can curl up and hide, protected by the dark" (271). But the convoluted odyssey, at once rectilinear and circular, of Magris's Ulyssiac character has to go on, accompanied by the affectivity of the household, at once present and transient. Encouraged by his children's voices, which had filled "his house, his days, his life" (277), the protagonist takes the leap into the unknown, into the most decisive experience of transit, that of trespass into a possible afterlife, in a hypothetical "home" or "Home" that, as in *You Will Therefore Understand*, is simultaneously a continuation and a hiatus with respect to his earthly abode.

Magris's fiction, however, tempers this apparently consolatory connection of life, space, and identity with disenchantment as a conceptual and ethical tool which, as we have seen in his essays, is a crucial component of his ironic, demystifying approach to false absolutes. His novel *Blindly*, written in 2005, is a compelling warning against the fetishization of geographic and emotional temporal dwellings and the inability or lack of determination to expose their dreadful "other" side, that of exile, deprivation, defenseless exclusion, not as metaphorical conditions but as real, de-humanizing experiences of loss.

As Tuan writes, "home is the focal point of a cosmic structure" (*Space* 149). Any human group considers "their own homeland as the center of the world. A people who believe they are at the center claim, implicitly, the ineluctable worth of their location" (149). But from the miniature *cosmos*, the ordered world of the little, self-contained habitats in *Microcosms*, the nocturnal prose of Magris's *Blindly* throws us into a destructive and self-destructive global *chaos*, a worldwide house of horrors enclosing the entire universe, where there is no room for a communitarian "we" but only for mutual violence, where boundaries are trespassed for lack of responsibility and of humanity.

4.2   Global unhomeliness: *Blindly*

> The world has lost its capacity to "form a world": it seems only to have gained that capacity of proliferating, to the extent of its means, the "unworld" [*immonde*], which, until now, and whatever one may think of retrospective illusions, has never in history impacted the totality of the orb to such an extent. (Nancy *Creation* 34)

French philosopher Jean-Luc Nancy's reflection on a socially disintegrated, unfair, uninhabitable world generated by globalization in contrast with the potential alternative of an authentic making of the world propelled by the struggle for justice can aptly introduce the concerns that Magris raises with his novel *Blindly*, where the "im-monde" (Nancy *Création* 16), a senseless "un-world" (*Creation* 34) soiled by injustice and discrimination manifests itself through an appalling worldwide display of human cruelty and misery. *Blindly* recounts the horrors and hopes of twentieth-century history and geography through the monologue of its fictional protagonist, who impersonates illegal immigrants, partisans, and fugitives across widely different lands and seas. In the protagonist's journey through ghastly places—from Tito's gulag on the Adriatic island of Goli Otok to the Nazi camps, from the Italo-Slavo-German territories of the Eastern border of Italy to the Spanish war, from the Iceland of a grotesque revolution to the Australia of convicts and emigrés—transience and mobility throughout the world mean only exclusion, suffering, and violence.

Although the novel's emphasis does not seem to be Europe as a philosophical and institutional project but rather a more global perspective on history, this literary tour de force in fact suggests equally forceful implications for the European legacy. Despite the need to distinguish between regressive and emancipatory forms of nationalism, Magris claims that, just as the idea of nation is a product of European culture, all nationalisms have a European origin, including those which react to European colonization ("Limes" 60). The universality of *Blindly* can hence be seen as an unrelenting attack on Europe's past horrors and as a warning against the risk of further physical and psychological sufferings that new "blind" political and institutional designs could cause not only outside but also inside European borders—what Étienne Balibar calls a "self-racization of Europe against itself" ("We" 44), a rejection of the "other" through an exasperation of intra-European differences. *Blindly* confronts us with the lack of the domestic or communitarian dimension due to the obliteration of those boundaries which, as Magris often reiterates, are necessary to delimit, hence to denote, to assign an identity—however multiple and unstable—to people and places. The anarchy of absolute drifting, without geographical, conceptual, or moral frontiers, overturns homeliness into its defamiliarizing other, literally, in Freudian terms, the *un-heimlich*, unhomely, showing precisely, as in the case of Freud's uncanny, the return of the repressed—the violence of Europe against its many "others," now coming back from the outside toward and against Europe itself.

An anticipation of this perverse reversal and of the need to speak up more forcefully about neglected aberrant pages of history can be found in the "Apsyrtides" chapter of *Microcosms*, where Goli Otok, initially introduced through the enticing rhetoric of a tourist brochure as "the island of peace, (…) an immaculate environment (…), an island of absolute freedom" (*Microcosms* 181), is fast overturned into "the final berth in a tragic odyssey undertaken by some of History's rejects" (181), of which the narrator offers a detailed synthesis.[8] After the Second World War, when a considerable portion of Italians living in Istria and Fiume (at the time belonging to Yugoslavia) relocated to Italy, about 2,000 workers from the town of Monfalcone, near Trieste, many of them committed antifascist, voluntarily moved to Yugoslavia with the desire to contribute to the construction of socialism, which they saw as the only hope of justice and equality. But when the Yugoslavian dictator Tito broke with Stalin, they remained faithful to the URSS and they were hence imprisoned as potentially dangerous conspirators, and tortured on the islands of Goli Otok and Sveti Grgur, together with war criminals, Yugoslavian Stalinists, and ordinary outlaws. If "a solitary island, an Eden on earth, can become a concentration camp for those who find themselves exposed to brutality with no means of defence" (187), and if individual nations remain silent about this horrific event, Magris with *Blindly* performs the task that the narrator in *Microcosms* urges, namely, "[t]o pluck this bloody footnote of world history from oblivion" (185) even without sharing those victims' political beliefs.

In his novel Magris interweaves the dreadful mishap of those unlucky Monfalconesi with equally appalling experiences of other people who, due to personal weakness or to challenging beliefs, found themselves "on the wrong side at the wrong time, out of place in History and in politics" (185) and had to undergo terrible suffering to resist annihilation. As Magris himself explains, the fictional first-person narrator and protagonist of the novel, Salvatore Cippico/Čipiko/Cipico, with his composite Italo-Slavic last name and his vicissitudes in two hemispheres, from his native Tasmania to a war-torn Spain, to Italian Fascism and Resistance, Dachau and Tito's gulag, is supposed to embody "one of those men who passed through the storms of History to end up in Goli Otok" (Magris "Making" 326). But the story of Salvatore's deportation to the Yugoslavian island overlaps and merges with that of other figures, with which Salvatore often identifies to the point of impersonating them. Among them is the Danish adventurer Jorgen Jorgensen, who seized power in Iceland for a few months before being jailed in Newgate Prison, and founded a settlement in Hobart Town, Tasmania, where he died. But also the mythical Jason is evoked in his quest for the Golden Fleece, with particular attention to the Argonauts' struggle with the Eastern barbarian Colchian population,[9] as an instance of the terrible clash of civilizations in which, Magris writes, the East—as in the case of the allegedly mysterious Eastern Europe identified with Communism—is "feared, scorned and rejected" ("Making" 327). Ultimately, Medea herself is relevant to *Blindly*, as her tragic conflict with Jason exemplifies the dialectics between creation and destruction in individual and collective relations, and also provides an archetype for the women that Salvatore loves and sacrifices in his adventures.

As we have read in *Microcosms*, a way of countering the fatal power of borders could be to feel and put oneself always on the other side. *Blindly* stages the drama caused by the inability or the lack of will to do so. In the global identitarian and cultural Babel of *Blindly*, even the places and thresholds that *Microcosms* depicts as welcoming habitats in which alterity is an intrinsic component of the individual and collective self manifest their most disturbing and shocking aspect. The city that in Magris's previous works represents at once the extension of domestic familiarity and openness to the unknown here loses its dual value and retains only a link with exclusion, suffering, and violence: "Every city is founded on blood" (*Blindly* 16). The universality of this "[b]utchery" (17) erases differences among areas of the world touched by the same devastation: "the aurora borealis and the aurora australis herald the same bloody sun (...). And it is so hard to tell anymore who is the barbarian (...), us or them" (17). Key topoi of Magris's poetics return, but twisted and debased by the global tragedy of history, of mankind's lack of measure and of respect of limits, be they geographical borders, institutional rules, or the laws of the heart—all those frontiers able precisely to open up dialogue instead of antagonizing people or letting unbridled power prevaricate unilaterally. The temporality of the home itself is now associated with images of surrogate dwellings doomed to destruction or icons of privation, which underscore nothing but the devastating side of precariousness, loss, and exile. Jails, concentration camps, prison-islands, makeshift hiding places, torturing chambers host the pain and horror of a mankind in disarray, impersonated by the multiple voices of an I that accompanies readers through total annihilation, including that of the records that could denounce the horror itself.

Like the characters in Magris's earlier fiction, also the official protagonist of *Blindly*, Salvatore, is "temporarily domiciled" (6), stationing in Trieste after being repatriated from Australia, and strategically juggles with false identities and dwelling places to escape the obsessive categorizations shared by authorities of prisons, psychiatric hospitals, and all other institutions that exert a disciplinary power over the individual, trying to reduce him to a univocal self. Not only is the spelling of his alleged name not always the same. The I who speaks had many "childhoods" (47) and takes on different identities, as his chaotic and fragmentary monologue unfolds—"I had other names as well (...) Yes 'Nevèra, Strijèla (...)" (20; 21). Salvatore shows off and then denies his own alienating plurality—"Jorgen Jorgensen, (...) John Johnson, no, Jan Jansen" (87–88). His self-estrangement also affects his physical features—"Sometimes I don't look like myself either" (37)—and his own voice, which sounds uncertain and even unrecognizable to him. By claiming that one "doesn't know what his voice sounds like; it's others who recognize it and distinguish it" (11) he hence acknowledges that there is no intrinsic truth or essence in his entire life, which is nothing more than "what others tell [him]" (191). Dissociated at the level of personality, as his psychiatrist's diagnosis confirms, and separated from his own voice, Salvatore is hence not only materially homeless but also dislodged from his own house of being.

Nevertheless, if this fragmentation may sound just like the character's self-complacency, a strategy to upset the psychiatrist who interrogates him at the mental health facility in Barcola, in fact it soon turns out to be the consequence of expulsion, imprisonments, and other shocking abuses dictated by ideological fanaticism. These dislocations condemn the individual to provisional homes and homelands that emerge as grotesque doubles of the temporary dwelling open to novelty as a possibility of enrichment: Newport prison, the mental hospital, Dachau's Lager, the gulag on the barren island of Goli Otok, and, in the best scenarios, hovels, holds, improvized beds, cellars, basements, an old granary. These alienating, makeshift abodes overturn not only the emotional foundations of Bachelard's poetics of domestic space, but, more radically, even the anthropological quality which, according to Marc Augé, renders space a place of identity and of relations, a "principle of meaning" (Augé *Non-places* 42) for dwellers and "a principle of intelligibility" (42) for observers. *Blindly*, in other words, transforms the space of the house into a "non-place" (63).

For Salvatore, who now impersonates the Danish adventurer Jorgen Jorgensen, the journey "down there" (*Blindly* 13) and the return "back down here, to the other side of the globe" (13), to his Tasmania which was also given different names, is an act of relocation and of renomination which, however, erodes the self rather than strengthen it. In the protagonist's perpetual escape, with "every move"—"trasloco" in the Italian original (*Alla cieca* 105)—something is lost, taken away. Yet, the principle underlying this progressive spoliation is not the positive logic of subtraction which, in Magris's identitarian theory, provides a momentary simplification to the self's multiplicity ("Identità" 520). *Microcosms* had ascribed this originary complexity not only to the Mitteleuropean condition but also to the subject in general, since "each identity is an aggregate and there is little sense in dismantling it so as to reach the supposed indivisible atom" (*Microcosms* 144). But Magris had also exposed the violent logic of identity *tout court*: "Every identity is also a horror, because it owes its existence to tracing a border and rebuffing whatever is on the other side" (38). *Blindly* is the tragedy of this exclusion, an amputation of the self and of all possible experience of domesticity.

As Tuan writes, "To be forcefully evicted from one's home and neighborhood is to be stripped of a sheathing, which in its familiarity protects the human being from the bewilderment of the outside world" (Tuan *Topophilia* 99). It is precisely the outside world, in all its hostility, that overpowers homeless Salvatore and condemns him to an alienating drifting. Expelled from Australia and back to Europe, he finds only temporary accommodation at his cousin's home in Fiume because in her turn the woman is thrown out of her house and has to be sheltered in a refugee camp at the Silos. Likewise, the abandonment of "our homes" (*Blindly* 23) in support of the socialist cause in Yugoslavia leads only to the discovery of an even narrower and atrocious space, the one behind bars, in the prison's "isolation cell" (25). When the I in the monologue impersonates Jorgen Jorgensen, its recollections degrade even the comfort of Iceland's royal palace, linking this luxurious dwelling to the Lager and the gulag. "[T]ransplanted to live and survive" (44) despite all the suffering and privations that he undergoes, the individual, according to Salvatore and to all the other *personae* he embodies, is hence, by definition, a "displaced person" (44; 131) who finds his only possible habitat in absolute *dépaysement*, to the point of disappearance—"Nowhere to be found" (131). Yet, once again, this condition of destructive errance is not glorified but rather presented as a denunciation, as an exemplary warning against what might otherwise stand out as the idyllic aspect of identity and culture as dislocation, and of exile as a simple metaphor.

The "temporary instability" (49) of dissidents, partisans, rebels, fugitives, and refugees also transforms their return to Europe into an infernal abyss. And the city that Jorgensen wants to create, "a bulwark of order and civilization at the edge of Emptiness" (94), is overturned into the chaos of burning Christiansborg. The fire that incinerates Jorgensen's urban homeland and his regal home does not simply exemplify sumptuary noble expenditure, the "magnificence of destruction, majesty that is resplendent in reducing everything to ashes" (60). It also connotes one of the many historical moments that in *Blindly* show how detachment, separation, and loss push the experience of transience to the frontiers of nothingness. When Jorgen boards the British collier, he leaves nothing behind, no locus of his infancy to which to come back. If, on the one hand, "the journey is the beginning of the return" (119), "*return*" in *Blindly* is a "strange word" (64), because, although danger and fatigue seem to dissolve when the journey "brings you back home" (65), the protagonist doubts that "houses to return to still exist" (65) or have ever existed. At times, the illusion prevails of not being an exile or a stranger, and of feeling at home in the entire world or among fellow prisoners.

Other passages nourish the hope for a return by evoking, for instance, the Croatian women patiently waiting for their men. Yet different scenes perversely dispute these reassuring images: the ice figurehead that the protagonist dreams of finding again after his departure from Iceland in fact melts, and, with it, also the prospect of reaching a harbor after years of traveling—"arrival in port is uncertain" (249). If in *Blindly* life is travel and, in particular "to live is to sail" (314), as the protagonist presumes, the purpose of this sea voyage is to transport and deport "stray" and "banished" exiles (252) deprived of their own homes, documents, and names.

The predicament of Salvatore and of his many alter egos, therefore, also offers a counterargument to Magris's claims in *L'infinito viaggiare*, where to travel means to discover the love for the whole world as for one's own home, and to come back to a home that is and has to be always different, so as to avoid the fetishism of domesticity (*Infinito* xi; xx). In light of the protagonist's drifting without definitive anchoring points, Cippico's claim that "if the proletarians of the world are united there are no more borders" (*Blindly* 219) and that the future of humanity will be international sounds tragically comic. Indeed, even if the flags "flow together" (347), hence giving the impression of a natural harmony among countries, the *pathos* of the border around which *Danube* and *Microcosms* revolve is here more central than ever. The Iron Curtain, "like a guillotine" (347), dissects Salvatore's heart. Not only is the love between him and Maria cut "in two like an apple" (277) by the political hostilities between Yugoslavia and Italy, one side falling on the side of freedom and one on the ground of dictatorship. The very body of the protagonist is "a violated border" (229). Referring to the tangle of intersecting nationalities, borders, and identities in the Mitteleuropean space, Magris had earlier depicted the frontier person as "himself a frontier, as if his own body were one of those no-man's lands between one border post and another, as if his own body had been scored and crossed by borderlines which unite and divide at the same time" ("Mitteleuropa" 143). The extreme violence and suffering that the characters in *Blindly* have to bear take this liminal identitarian condition to extremes, in a catastrophic literalization of what Étienne Balibar has conceptualized as the defamiliarizing shift from the nation–states having borders to the citizen being a border (*Politics* 83–84), from the static idea of fixed lines of territorial demarcation to a protean status inseparable from the citizen's own mobility and self-alienation.

At the epilogue of his recollection, Salvatore–Jorgensen, the spokesperson for all the other tormented and displaced Argonauts of the novel, seems to find an apparent shelter in a providential homecoming, which, however, is immediately perturbed by the recognition of fear: "I'm afraid to go home" (341). The domestic environment that receives him, far from comforting, generates increasing insecurity and uneasiness, ultimately culminating with the shock at his woman's horrific trespass. In "the freezing hovel" (341), Norah's welcome is crude, beastly. Rather than the warmth of the heart and of the hearth, it evokes violence, fury, and ultimately death itself. And if the earth could at first be taken as a home on a larger scale, Salvatore's words deprive it of stability and security by assimilating it to "a ship floating above a watery abyss" (353), and ultimately to the space of damnation, where "hells are found" (354).

Although to make history means "to bring order to the jungle, to map out paths and roads through the indistinct marsh" (290), *Blindly* ultimately envisions total erasure of both static and mobile abodes, households of the body and of the soul alike, as the only radical way out of the endless suffering caused by seclusion, escape, and exile. Identity, the Danubian traveler had written, "is partly made up of places, of the streets where we have lived and left part of ourselves" (*Danube* 215). In the final pages of *Blindly*, however, Salvatore's attempt to burn all laws and documents, and the possible technological glitch that deletes data and computer messages convey a desire to annihilate the memories of all the atrocious dwelling places that maimed the self with the marks of injustice and privation. In *Microcosms* the sea "teaches the freedom to recognize oneself as having been vanquished" (*Microcosms* 181), and frees us from the obsessive "longing for affirmation and victory" (181). Yet in *Blindly* not even the hope for an ultimate escape by sea can be lifesaving for Salvatore, as the sea becomes "a sudarium" (*Blindly* 366), a figure of agony and death, the only possible evasion not recorded by classificatory writing.

But this withdrawal from life and representability, this apparent final act of blindness, in fact does not weaken the urgent need to bear witness to this choral drama of misery and pain. All the oppressed and oppressors of the novel who exile themselves from the scene of the story reenter the stage of history through the plot. They continue to dwell in the literary narrative, that temporary home to which Magris's traveler–author comes back between journeys in order to fill the "blank spaces" (*Danube* 35) of existence, enjoying the domestic intimacy of "the objects in the room" (35). In *Blindly*, this existence is not only Salvatore's but also that of all those weak and damned beings, losers, and scapegoats, who ask for a voice after paying for the crazy aspirations of individual and collective power, and toward whom that very power turned a blind eye. This voice cannot but be deranged and chaotic, a "violent whirlpool of words" ("Making" 330) that "suffocates the self who utters it" (330), as it has to reflect a frightening irrationality. In the contemporary novel—Magris has recently written in *La letteratura è la mia vendetta*—the narrator who wants to find Ariadne's thread in the story s/he is telling has constantly to run the risk of losing that thread, that is, has to come to terms with discontinuity and disorder (*Vendetta* 19). *Blindly* morphs not only language but also dwelling places into labyrinthine geographical and historical settings where Ariadne's thread ends in a tangle. It hence substantiates Magris's claim that the truth of life can be fully grasped only in the experiences of characters who have to pass through disorder and delirium (*Vendetta* 14; 17).

"*To create the world*" (Nancy *Creation* 54), Nancy writes, "means immediately, without delay, reopening each possible struggle for a world, that is, for what must form the contrary of a global injustice against the background of general equivalence" (54). *Blindly* is Magris's own act of *mondialisation*, of world-forming against an *im-monde*, which he connotes in terms uncannily similar to Nancy's as "an indifferentiated equivalence of everything with everything else" (Magris *Storia* 16). Facing this history of terrifying wrongdoing and indifference inscribed in the past of European nations, and the equally alarming potential of future reiterations, the challenge that *Blindly* leaves us is to create what in the essay "Patria e identità" [Homeland and identity] Magris defines as "a habitable dwelling in life, (...) a reality in which to feel at home in the world" (*Storia* 160), where individuals and communities can recognize their diversity. The existence and the dignity of Europe lie in Europe's ability to become that provisional, plural but unavoidable home delivered from injustice and oppression which, like Ernst Bloch's ideal homeland as the real birth house of life (160), nobody has ever inhabited so far, because it is a world that does not exist yet.

Notes

1 Although Benjamin coined the term *Denkbild*, it is Adorno who elaborated on this new discursive form and philosophical investigation which, as thought, language, image, and dream at once, welds together objective criticism and

subjective experiences. See Adorno, "Benjamin's *Einbahnstrasse*" 323; Stevens and Hardick Weston "Free Time" 137–140. "Microscopic" is another key definition that in most critics qualifies Benjamin's approach to representation. See Buck-Morss *Origin* 74; Sontag "Introduction" *One Way* 19–20; Eagleton, *Ideology* 328–329.

2 The following passages from "Marseilles" and "Moscow" exemplify Benjamin's technique and its affinity with Magris's own style: "Unfathomable wetness that swills from the upper tier, in a dirty, cleansing flood over dirty planks and warty mountains of pink shellfish, bubbles between the thighs and bellies of glazed Buddhas, past yellow domes of lemons, into the marshlands of cresses and through the woods of French pennants, finally to irrigate the palate as the best sauce for the quivering creatures (...)—all this is incessantly sieved, grouped, counted, cracked open, thrown away, prepared, tasted. And the slow, stupid agent of inland trade, paper, has no place in the unfettered element, the breakers of foaming lips that forever surge against the streaming steps" ("Marseilles" *One Way* 212).

"Travel by streetcar in Moscow is above all a tactical experience. Here the newcomer learns perhaps most quickly of all to adapt himself to the curios tempo of this city and to the rhythm of its peasant population. And the complete interpenetration of technological and primitive modes of life, this world-historical experiment in the new Russia, is illustrated in miniature by a streetcar ride" ("Moscow" *One Way* 190). Likewise, "The Pastry Cook from children's fairy tales seems to have survived only in Moscow. Only here are there structures made of nothing but spun sugar, sweet icicles with which the tongue indemnifies itself against the bitter cold. Most intimately of all, snow and flowers are united in candy icing; there at last the marzipan flora seems to have fulfilled entirely Moscow's dream, to bloom out of whiteness" (193).

3 Given its centrality in Benjamin's cultural and philosophical vision, this approach to space and subjectivity has been the object of numerous critical works, among which Gilloch *Benjamin* 87–112; Latham "City."

4 The impersonal narrative voice of *Microcosmi* veils, in fact, specific events of the author's life, which enhance the homely ambiance of the book. For instance, Magris's autobiographical details emerge from the apparently general remarks about "that table where one had studied for the German literature exam and now, many years later, one wrote or responded to yet another interview about Trieste, its *Mitteleuropa* culture and its decline, while not far away one son is correcting his degree dissertation and another, in the end-room, is playing cards" (*Microcosms* 6).

5 Evidence that this metaphor is not simply an aesthetic notation but, rather, a geopolitical and ethical principle can be found in the essay "Considerazioni di frontiera," where Magris expresses his attraction to "trascolorare" (*Utopia* 63) precisely in connection with the indefiniteness and permeability of borders.

6 The specific domestic reference in the original Italian expression, "felice dimora" (*Microcosmi* Garzanti 153), is lost in the English translation, which renders it as "the place of happiness" (*Microcosms* 153).

7 In his more recent book-length interview *La vita non è innocente*, Magris connects the two contexts with an explicit reference to *Microcosms*, presenting both of them as places with open doors, where one goes to sit for a moment in front of an old image. Magris explains the strong proximity he feels of church and tavern, bread and wine, as signs of a Rothian sense of Christianity (*Vita* 29).

8 References to Goli Otok already appear in *A Different Sea*, which confirms the very long gestation of *Blindly*, to which Magris often refers in his interviews.

9 For a discussion of the myth of Jason in *Blindly* see Parmegiani "Presence"; Appel "Plowing."

5
Habitat and Habitus

Abstract: *This chapter focuses on the ethical function of literature in Magris's most recent and still untranslated essay collections (*La storia non è finita, Livelli di guardia, La vita non è innocente, Letteratura e ideologia, La letteratura è la mia vendetta, Segreti e no*), which contextualize in contemporary society the historical, political, and philosophical issues that Magris addresses in his fiction. Writing for Magris is a form of relocation, an adventure toward an unattainable promised homeland, which makes us feel simultaneously in the unknown and at home but with the awareness of not owning a home. A comparative exploration of the secret in Magris and Derrida shows how, unlike deconstruction, precariousness ascribes to the writer the responsibility to look for meaning and to defend shareable principles and values able to promote tolerance and pluralism—to build what Magris defines as a liveable dwelling in life, a habitable collective reality where individuals and communities can recognize and respect their diversity.*

Keywords: civility; Claudio Magris and values; democracy and tolerance; Jacques Derrida and the secret; literature and ethics; Mario Vargas Llosa

Pireddu, Nicoletta. *The Works of Claudio Magris: Temporary Homes, Mobile Identities, European Borders.* New York: Palgrave Macmillan, 2015.
DOI: 10.1057/9781137488046.0008.

5.1 The essayist and the tortoise

> In the present unreality of the world, it is increasingly difficult to answer Nietzsche's question: "Where can I feel at home?" (Magris *Utopia* 65)

As cultural anthropologist James Clifford observes, the moment traveling becomes a cultural practice, dwelling can no longer be conceived simply as "the ground from which traveling departs, and to which it returns" (Clifford "Traveling" 115). There is always a shore lapped by Magris's sea, and there is always a land that makes border crossing possible in Magris's literary travels, yet the *status viatoris* of Magris's character is like that of Marisa in *Microcosms*, who "comes out of the water—the first time, the hundredth time" (*Microcosms* 156) in a "inexhaustible and unexplainable" sea (156). And, above all, there is always an abode that can make the self feel temporarily at home while traveling or yielding to the sea tide, but it is a home where love of distance and love of the hearth coincide (*Infinito* xx), a home, hence, that makes us feel like foreigners in life within one's own domestic walls.

Against the danger of endogamy and of the defense of pure identity, Magris reminds us that blood is always "meticcio" (*Utopia* 69), hybrid, as the Danube itself confirms through its cultural and ethnic "meticce metamorfosi" (*Danubio* Garzanti 1999: 15) [hybrid metamorphoses]. However, although hybridity in Magris dislocates the individual from the private abode of self-sameness and across the borders of homeland, it does not lead to the diasporic identity produced by a leveling globalization, and not even to the generalized *métissage* proposed, among other postcolonial critics, by Édouard Glissant, for whom hybridization and creolization without frontiers become a "self-conscious, general *principle*" (Glissant *Poetics* 46) involving the entire world. Although Magris endorses the thought of the Antillean writer, his own *métissage* does not intend to dilute the specificity of the European ideal. A united Europe, possibly a veritable state itself—decentered through federalism yet politically and juridically unified[1]—is precisely what he sees as a defense against the disappearance of its internal diversity. An authentic worldwide culture, for him, is predicated upon different forms and languages that are all joint manifestations of human universality, yet Europe should not lose the sense of its own differentiated and variegated unity (Magris and Ciccarelli 422). Europe should incorporate the sense of the limit ("Limes" 55)—a founding element of its identity according to Magris—while preventing new frontiers and new walls from being erected, be they ethnic, chauvinistic, or particularistic ones (*Utopia* 64).

As he rejects the vision of a European space and consciousness dissolving into a universal bazaar—a recurring expression which, in his writings, connotes the chaotic indistinction of globalization—Magris hence also provides a powerful counterdiscourse to other intellectuals' denunciation of the impossible ambivalence of what I would call a European post-national hetero-identity. For Jacques Derrida, the demise of Europe as cape, headland, and heading of world civilization (*Other* 20) is also that of the border as a univocal geopolitical and spiritual concept. The cultural identity of a new Europe whose borders are no longer given has to answer to a "double injunction" (44): "not to reconstitute a centralizing hegemony but also not to multiply the borders, the movements and margins, not to cultivate for their own sake minority differences, untranslatable idiolects [or] national antagonisms" (44). Confronted with this complex scenario in which frontiers ask the European identity to be equal *to itself and to the other*" (45), Derrida presents this new European crisis and responsibility as the "experience and experiment of the impossible" (45). Along the same line, Étienne Balibar concludes that "[t]here is no more Europe" or less and less of its essence or substance" (*Politics* 100).

For his part, animated by what he presents as the optimism of the will ("Limes" 72), Magris accepts the challenge of this alleged impossibility and defends the specificity of the European legacy. Europe, for him, distinguishes itself from other cultures like that of America or of the Orient for its "peculiar relationship with the individual and the whole. It's a society in which the emphasis has always been placed on the individual, but not in an anarchic way" (Magris and Zucchini). The European heritage brings the individual to a "progressive self-interest in which the 'I' also encompasses the community" (Magris and Zucchini). It is hence upon these principles that Magris supports the feasibility of a united Europe, without neglecting the problems and contradictions in this project. Indeed, as he writes in "The Fair of Tolerance," the "principle of equal dignity and equal rights for all men (...) presupposes a reciprocal tolerance of differences and dialogue between cultures" ("Fair"). Although the unification of Europe marks an important step toward "an extension of the dialogue and the feeling of belonging together" ("Fair"), Magris remarks that this unavoidable premise of civilization is also being put to test within united Europe itself, which, by increasingly hosting new peoples and cultures, is confronting practices and values conflicting with its own. Magris believes that

[t]he peoples coming from other cultures will have to become European yet still retain their distinctiveness, not be brutally standardised to our model. Only if Europe is capable of carrying out this task resolutely and open-mindedly will it continue to develop, in a new form, the great role it has played in world history. We should not deceive ourselves that it will be an easy task, and that the obstacles to this process will spring solely from retrograde narrow-mindedness or obtuse racism. Only if the objective difficulties are not underrated can one hope to overcome them. ("Fair")

In the contemporary intellectual panorama, Europe's self-theorization seems to have reached a conceptual dead-end because to devise a new Europe able to shun both monopoly and dispersion (Derrida *Other* 41) means to think what is difficult to imagine, as also Balibar claims (Balibar *Politics* 88). Yet, Magris shows us that it is possible and more productive to imagine what is difficult to think, that is, to entrust to the creative power of literature to construct what abstract speculation fails to accomplish. Conscious of the risk of mere "literary complacency" ("Debate" 79), with his writings he creates a "European social imaginary" (79) which, without assuming to find readymade solutions in literature, can draw from it the inspiration to continue exploring ways to make the European ideal part of the real life of people.

His intellectual and creative engagement through literature extends beyond his commitment to the European ideal. Just like Salvatore in *Blindly*, the writer with "a pen in hand [is] History" (*Blindly* 324), a History and a story he creates as a "frontier man" (*Utopia* 62) endlessly articulating and undoing new meanings and values. Every literary expression, for Magris, "is a threshold" (*Utopia* 62) that operates at multiple frontiers, building some and destroying others, and teaches us to trespass limits while simultaneously moving and redrawing them in different contexts. Magris has repeatedly connoted the traveler as somebody who in his journeys takes his entire life with him, "like a tortoise that travels together with its own house" (*Infinito* xii), or like the literary figure of the Oriental Jew who, apparently deprived of a land and of frontiers, "has his own homeland within himself" (*Utopia* 61) hence is "never far from home" (62). This connection between self, movement, and home informs the voyage of the word as well. Writing for Magris is an adventure toward an unattainable promised homeland, but it is precisely this precariousness that ascribes to the writer the responsibility to create shareable principles able to promote tolerance and pluralism.

Magris's aesthetic and ethical vision enacts the premises of what Zygmunt Bauman (drawing from Richard Sennet's definition) presents as "civility" (Bauman *Modernity* 95), that is, sociability without the interference of power and of the overload of personal feelings. "Civility, like language, cannot be 'private'" (95), Bauman underlines. This implies not only giving priority to the social dimension over individualism, but also to transcend the coldness and indifference of what is merely "public," that is, a collective experience "stripped of the challenge of 'togetherness' it contains, with its standing invitation to meaningful encounter, dialogue and interaction" (105). Through the civil language of his fiction and essays, Magris promotes what Bauman endorses as the "ability to live with differences, (…) and to benefit from it, (…) the art of negotiating common interests and shared destiny" (106), instead of hiding "in the shelters of communal uniformity, monotony and repetitiveness" (106). All the more reason, civility can be considered the foundation of Magris's vision of Europe, favoring "interaction with strangers without holding their strangeness against them" (104), and striving to overcome the tendency to seek "security in a common identity" (106) for fear or "inability to face up to the vexing plurality of human beings" (106).

Without renouncing projectuality, Magris's writings ultimately urge us to accept the frontiers of identities, territories, and cultures yet with the awareness of their relativity, just as we accept the borders of our temporary and mobile dwelling place between the window of one's own home and the world (*Utopia* 61, 67), like Novalis's wandering hero, immersed in the endless flux of becoming but always homeward bound. It is this quest for balance and moderation that inspires Magris to address the relationship between the private and the public domains in his most recent collections of essays on social and civic issues. Magris's critical engagement focuses on what I propose to define as the interplay between the allegedly continuous space of individual identity—the self's *habitat*—and *habitus*—a set of behaviors, practices, and beliefs produced and reproduced in society and culture without conscious links with their historical origins or rational purposes.[2]

Magris's essays examine the collective perceptions and discourses generated by these acquired dispositions, concentrating in particular on the ethical underpinnings of such ingrained mindsets and activities when the stakes are not just innocuous tastes and feelings but, in fact, the foundational principles and values of individual and collective life. The target of Magris's criticism is, we could say, the moral numbness that legitimizes behavioral and thinking patterns disrespectful of the basic norms of civility. As he undermines commonly accepted yet questionable customs and judgments generated and perpetuated by a complacent socio-political scenario, Magris emphasizes the need for individual agency and responsibility. The citizen, and *a fortiori* the writer, should be neither an autarchic dweller divorced from the *polis* nor a participant in the dull conformism of what Magris defines as a "gelatinous middle class" (*Democrazia* 16), intellectually uninvolved hence unable or unwilling to renew ideas. With his essays, Magris attacks, and invites readers to reject, a degrading collective *habitus* which, out of convenience or of simple ignorance caused by cultural flattening, has crystallized perceptions and behaviors, making it difficult to distinguish between subtle conditioning and authentic freedom of thought and action. Convinced, like Tuan, that we are "tenants of the earth" (*Space* 7), Magris shares with him a concern "with the design of a more human habitat" (7), and his essays respond to it by promoting liberal thinking in the original Stoic sense of freedom of the mind from the constraints of habit and conventions.

5.2 Edifices of values

Since its popularization by Michel de Montaigne, the essay has been considered a literary genre undertaking an inquiry that weighs, tests thoughts on a particular subject, rather than ostentatiously and authoritatively asserting a subjective point of view. Magris represents the quintessential essayist because he exposes his ideas "in the form of an absolute striving" (Harrison, *Essayism* 3). He highlights the challenges undermining each intellectual endeavor, and subjects his convictions to the critical filter of doubt and irony, away from extremism and always conscious of the tension between unity and chaos. The words that Magris adopts in *Danube* to describe Georg Lukács's essayistic activity aptly summarize the principles of his own cognitive quest:

> the essayist's craft displays the agonizing, ironical vicissitudes of the intellect which is aware how far immediacy lacks authenticity, and how far life diverges from its meaning; and yet the intellect aims, however obliquely, at that ultimately unattainable transcendence of meaning—whose flickering presence is to be seen in the very awareness of its absence. (*Danube* 262)

From the volumes *La storia non è finita* [History Has Not Ended] (2006) and *Livelli di guardia* [Danger Levels] (2011)—which collect essays that Magris mostly wrote in the last decade for *Corriere della Sera* on political and social issues pertaining to contemporary Italy, Europe, and the West at large—to the short books *La vita non è innocente* [Life is not Innocent] (2008),

Democrazia, legge e coscienza [Democracy, Law and Conscience] (2010), and *Segreti e no* (2014) [Secrets and Non Secrets], the idea of domestic threshold becomes the demarcating line between what is ethically acceptable according to individual and collective principles and what trespasses boundaries. These books reinforce the main topoi that inform his fiction, but Magris here dons his diurnal garb, that of the systematic intellectual who, through lucid and provocative argumentations, is not afraid of reviving moral questions. As Marco Alloni observes in his introduction to *La vita non è innocente*, Magris rehabilitates morality from a downgraded expression of naivete to a much needed contemporary value (*Vita* 6) for the preservation of human dignity.

In a world in which secularism clashes with fundamentalism, Magris, for instance, tackles the question of "laicità" (*Storia* 25–30) [laicism], presenting it as a mental critical attitude allowing one to distinguish that which is rationally demonstrable from objects of faith, so as to delimit their respective competencies according to rules and logical principles free from the influence of any religious creed or ideology. Laicism hence implies "tolerance, doubt even towards our own certainties, self-irony, demystification of all idols, including our own" (*Storia* 26), without confusing rigorous thought with fanatical convictions and authentic feelings with visceral emotional reactions. Magris's approach is in line with Franco Cassano's treatment of lay culture as "a deconstruction of fundamentalisms, and a demilitarized reading of one's own tradition" (Cassano *Southern* xlvii). Laic for Magris is whoever "can adhere to an idea without submitting to it" (*Storia* 26), free from the need to both "worship and desecrate" (26), hence detached from both intrusive clericalism and radical pseudo-culture. A model for this balanced approach able to separate morals and rights, concepts and passions, is offered by the thought of Italian intellectual Norberto Bobbio.[3] Magris repeatedly discusses Bobbio's philosophical, juridical, and political engagement as an effective resistance to what for him is a growing "conceptual and moral illiteracy" (*Storia* 33) which, in a worrisome obscurantism, confuses victims and culprits and erases the accomplishments of a liberal culture that used to provide guarantees and control mechanisms able to prevent power abuses. Agreeing with another alleged master of laicism, namely, the German philosopher Max Weber, Magris in *Livelli di guardia* concludes that, although each of us contributes a particular vision of things, hence an individual truth, its effects depend on how such a truth is presented. A laic declares his convictions trying not to influence his/her interlocutors and putting him/herself at stake. By contrast, whoever arrogantly asserts truth once and for all is intolerant, totalitarian, and clerical (*Livelli* 68).

Magris shows that this problem of limits, hence once again of borders, affects, in particular, Italy's political struggles. Substantiating his claims with his short-lived political involvement as a senator from 1994 to 1996, Magris no longer sees healthy clashes between different forces and opinions able to resort to the art of compromise, if necessary, yet without trespassing acceptable "frontiers of decency" (*Storia* 166). Rather, he maintains that Italian politics has perverted its original functions because the foundation of each state or human community, namely, the equality before the law, has been debased to a network of partisan, or even personal, interests. Magris is conscious of the risk of sounding moralizing, yet he responds to this potential critique by underlining that politics cannot be made with immorality. On this premise, he considers the current deterioration of political practices a consequence of a more radical, alarming phenomenon, namely, the disappearance of the elementary rules of civil life. For instance, he maintains that the by-now customary use of foul language in Italian political exchanges is not simply a demonstration of rudeness but, more profoundly, the sign of a substantial lack of the attitude that Kant presented as the basis of any other virtue, namely, respect, the guarantor of "the sense of our own dignity and that of others" (*Livelli* 149) at the roots of every civilization and correct interpersonal relationship.

The real scandal, for Magris, lies in the fact that the politicians' inappropriate conduct and expressions do not stir public outrage. Echoing Dostoevsky's chilling prophecy of a world where everything is permitted, Magris hence recalls, for instance, the invitation of a serial killer as a special guest in a prime-time television show on the Italian national TV network, an episode which prompts him to reflect upon the gleeful indifference with which evil is banalized and spectacularized in contemporary society (*Storia* 125). On the one hand, Magris asserts that nobody, not even a ruthless criminal, should be considered only the author of his/her offenses. In other words, anyone is, above all, an individual. On the other hand, however, what makes an individual interesting is his/her humanity—not *because of*, but, rather, *despite* the evil he/she committed. "Evil is interesting only when it is mixed up and ambiguously intertwines with good, in the demonic contradictions of existence" (126), precisely the contradictions that Magris continues to explore through his fiction and non-fiction works.

Most interventions in *La storia non è finita* and *Livelli di guardia* contribute to a wider meditation on the fundamental values of democracy, freedom, and action, their relationship with the law, and their trivializations and manipulations in a degraded Western social and political ambiance that is reaching global proportions and increasingly ignoring the principle of responsibility. It is unquestionable that Magris upholds the European origin of those values, substantially aligning himself with what also the preamble of the never ratified European Constitution presents as the spiritual and intellectual legacy of the Old Continent.[4] Yet his passionate defense of the principle of universal value leads him to address the problem of its deterioration not only in the Eurocentric past but also in the allegedly democratic and tolerant European present. Drawing from Max Weber's opposition between an ethics of conviction and an ethics of responsibility, Magris distinguishes action that obeys only to one's own principles, regardless of their consequences, from action not inspired uniquely by personal values but also able to consider wider implications beyond the sphere of one's own particularities. Responsibility for Magris means readiness to pay the price and to accept the renunciations that each deed requires without attempting to have our own cake and eat it, too (*Storia* 66–67).

It is precisely the disappearance of this crucial disposition that Magris denounces in what for him has become a "slimy social totality" (*Livelli* 197) which, propelled by populism, has destroyed "every sentiment of what is permissible or not" (197). As he claims equally poignantly in *La storia non è finita*, in that "universal bazaar of our world everything is (...) questionable, negotiable, possible" (*Storia* 125), as though, for instance, solidarity or racism could be interchangeable commodities displayed side by side in a window shop and in the consumers' minds like opinions in newspapers. Magris thus consolidates the image of the contemporary social and ethical scenario that in *Utopia e disincanto* he had defined as "the era of the optional" (*Utopia* 265), regulated by the "stock-exchange of values" (257), namely, a cultural climate where it is becoming more and more difficult to define ourselves in a precise, hence limited way so as to choose one thing and exclude other ones. Everything for Magris now seems to be reduced to an element that can be accepted or refused at one's own leisure without facing the alternative between complete adhesion or rejection. From a standpoint that counters a philosophical postmodern approach like, for instance, that of Italian pensie-ro *debole* [weak thought],[5] Magris states that only "a strong thought, able to establish hierarchies of values" (*Utopia* 259) can guarantee freedom to individuals because it endows them with the power to choose, and to resist the factory of opinions and slogans managed by the "soft and colloidal totalitarianism of mediatic power" (259). Dostoevsky, in his view, makes us face *the* crucial question, namely, whether or not to give up the need for, and the problem of value. But the refusal to engage with this dilemma, for Magris, would be naive, as he has always expressed his opposition to any attempt to reduce the issue of value to "a pathetic and outmoded nostalgia, or to a repressive self-punishment" (Magris *Quale totalità* 67). Only in the framework of this need is it possible to consider the possibility of transgression.

These are topics that Magris continues to discuss in shorter texts, such as *Democrazia, legge e coscienza* (2010), co-authored with Italian art critic Stefano Levi della Torre, and the long interview collected in book form by Marco Alloni as *La vita non è innocente* (2008). Magris's collaboration with other intellectuals (more instances will be discussed in section ii) further reinforces his attempt to transcend the separation between the individual sphere (hence *a fortiori* that of the isolated writer, enclosed within his private cultural dwelling) and the community. The dialogical format of these works posits the need for a common ground where ideas can be shared on crucial issues for the well-being of the *polis*, without imposing one's own truth but, rather, looking for truth as a journey with others. Therefore, the term "co-scienza" [conscience], so frequent in his reflections, can be treated, etymologically, as *cum-scio*, a cognitive experience lived together with someone else. By rendering our quest for knowledge and truth a shareable undertaking, each of us can engage in a critical exchange which makes us face the complexity of human relations, notions and values, but also encourages us to persevere in our search.

Starting from the interpretation of individual conscience as the collective voice of an ideal ethical community to which we feel we belong, Magris in *Democrazia, legge e coscienza*, lingers on the conflict between law and conscience, the tragic laceration embodied by the Greek literary figure of Antigone. Caught between the unwritten divine laws and the positive laws of the state promulgated by Creon, Sophocle's heroine sacrifices herself in the name of universal values and absolute principles rather than submit to the authority of unjust codified laws.[6] Although democracy represents a legitimately elected majority, Magris defends the individual's right to revolt against its laws if they go against "principles that transcend the contingency and relativity of that particular historical moment and of the socio-political structure" (*Democrazia* 7). Yet, he maintains that it is only a "false democracy" (20) that generates this conflict or that eliminates the dialectics between law and conscience whenever the law is allowed passively to adjust to the practices of a specific historical moment or to the evolution of reality without authentically confronting the underlying problems.[7] What Magris perceives as a totalitarian elimination of any tension between high and low, order and chaos, life and death, meaning and nothingness, is the result of a relativism which, by rendering everything interchangeable, leads to the triumph of apathy and ultimately favors hegemony instead of guaranteeing freedom. In Magris's argumentation, the law thus represents an indispensible threshold defining the individual and society, hence corroborating Magris's idea of the necessity of frontiers. They *can* and at times *have to* be contested or even trespassed, but always responsibly, according to one's own conscience, and should never be violated or ignored.

Therefore, the so-called edifice of one's own values (11) should be neither closed in on itself nor wide open. The "continuing, humble, adogmatic search for hierarchies of values" (*Utopia* 260) that Magris had posited in *Utopia e disincanto* as the only answer to the centrifugal drive of indifference takes center stage in *La vita non è innocente*, where it authenticates his reflections by connecting them to decisive turns and major difficulties in his personal path. It is in his household, in his family context, that—Magris avows—he learned to appreciate loyalty as a "non-dogmatic sense of coherence" (*Vita* 14) and the indispensability of respect, because "respect is that which demonstrates the sense of everyone's sacredness" (16). The individual, however, is never exempt from responsibility. Magris avows that he experiences responsibility as that paradoxical feeling of culpability which renders Josef K, the protagonist of Kafka's "The Trial," guilty precisely because he does not want to acknowledge his guilt. Magris hence concludes that life is not innocent, as we all inhabit and participate in a world where there are injustice, violence, evil. Even if we are not individually guilty of the world's evil, none of us can be unconcerned. Our inevitable involvement in contexts much bigger than ourselves also throws light upon the importance of the past and tradition in Magris, for both literary activity and personal relationships. Through the continuity granted by what he defines as the "ethics of memory" (53), all that has value, be it a passion or a person, remains present even beyond death. This strong sense of community between the living and the dead derives from Magris's belief in the effectiveness of history, of the concreteness provided by historicity as a protection against the pure abstraction of rhetoric.

Magris's overall vision tinges life with an epic quality born of incessant, never mastered challenges that prevent individuals from completing their journey and feeling at home, ready to close the door. First of all, life for Magris is a compromise, not to be intended in its negative sense of a concession to a derogatory situation, but, rather, as a combination of things we passionately believe in and of more unpleasant but unavoidable ones that we have to accept (*Vita* 46–47). But, above all, life is inconsistent, a constant blend of sense and nonsense, of authenticity and ambiguity in big and small things, without a clear distinction. In Magris's short book *Segreti e no* [Secrets and Non Secrets] (2014), this ambiguous and contradictory condition, which makes individuals aware of their precariousness and of the need to avoid the extremism of both anarchy and idolatry, is epitomized, more specifically, by the logic of the secret. Exploring the tension between concealing and revealing secrets in the public sphere, Magris discusses different areas, from politics to esoteric cultures, in which the secret embodies power itself by rendering truth unattainable. Although Magris questions the mystifying, manipulative custody of the secret as a "sacral interdiction" (*Segreti* 21) that restricts access to a superior truth only to a few initiated, he draws attention to the purported clarity and visibility of mysteries in major religions, concluding that unnecessary obscurity is a falsification and profanation of what for him is the deep mystery of life's simple, everyday being.

Nevertheless, if the home is an "intimate place" (Tuan *Space* 144) providing spatial and emotional proximity, dwelling in *Segreti e no* defines a space of privacy where not even our apparently simple everyday life is transparent and unproblematic. Not only does possession of a hidden truth confer on the individual an "irreducible peculiarity" (*Segreti* 9) ungraspable by others, but also each of us is a custodian of a secret, that of our most profound identity, "so secret that it is even unknown to ourselves" (11). Although Magris does not develop systematically his reflections on the inscrutability of the self,[8] his book raises an issue that Jacques Derrida, for instance, has tackled in several of his works (*A Taste for the Secret*, *Given Time*, *Passions*, among many others), namely, the role of what is hidden or veiled in the tension between presence and absence that characterizes his approach to knowability. Starting from this common element, we can grasp the implications of the two authors' respective approaches to the status of truth, the production of meaning, the conceptualization of identity, and the role of responsibility. To unveil a secret, to bring it to light, for Magris always means also to deform it, for the very fact that it is inserted into a different context. This coexistence of transparency and opacity is precisely what leads Derrida to claim that even in consensus "the secret is never broached/breached" (Derrida *Taste* 57), because the pre-requisite for sharing, communication, and thematization is "that there be something non-thematizable, non-objectifiable, non-sharable. And this 'something' is an absolute secret, it is the *ab-solutum*" (57), etymologically "cut off from any bond, detached" (57). Therefore, to speak *of* the secret without being able to *say* it means, for Derrida, to enact the "sharing of what is not shared" (58). In other words, "we know in common that we have nothing in common" (58) and the only possible consensus pertains to the fact that "the singular is singular, that the other is other, that *tout autre est tout autre*" (58).

Disclosure of a secret for Derrida would entail the end of meaning, because nothing else could be said. With its semantic inexhaustibility, the secret hence exhibits the endless drifting of signifiers corresponding to the Derridian concept of *différance*—at once difference and deferral of meaning, without positive terms—but also of *différend*—the dissension and lack of agreement and of order generated by the absence of shareable content. For Derrida, this paradoxical dimension is embodied by the autobiographical realm (57), insofar as the self is the locus of unknowability and lack of consensus *par excellence*. Likewise, Magris's treatment of the secret as a sign of the impenetrability of the self substantiates his notion of an ungraspable identity that manifests itself as spatio-temporal mobility. For both intellectuals, the space of the secret defines alterity as "not-belonging" (59), which also implies responsibility to the other: "the fact of avowing one's belonging, of putting in common—be it family, nation, tongue—spells the loss of the secret" (59). For Magris each of us is always other and located on the other side. For Derrida, the secret is, etymologically, separation (*secernere*), hence creation of a private dimension of alterity and heterogeneity. Yet the indecipherable and enigmatic nature of the secret questions not only the totality of meaning and the conquest of truth but also the power of authority. By conceptualizing the secret as a space of inviolability, Derrida brings up the issue of "political ethics" (59) and, opposing "the demand that everything be paraded in the public square" (59), claims that "if a right to the secret is not maintained, we are in a totalitarian space" (59). Likewise, while recognizing the increasing difficulties reconciling the defence of the individual from abusive invasions of privacy with the legitimate protective measures against threats to the community and the state, Magris defends the inalienability of "a space of one's own where to be free from everything and everyone" (Magris *Segreti* 36), in line with what Édouard Glissant presents as "the right to opacity, to protect the deepest recesses of one's being and feelings from the X-rays of any global knowledge" (35–36).

The "totalitarianization of democracy" (Derrida *Taste* 59), which for Derrida annihilates the space of the secret in the name of "public expression, exhibition, phenomenality" (59) also throws light on both authors' conceptualization of the function of literature. Derrida provocatively claims that any literary work or form of writing is a crime and even perjury, because if the message is readable, the secret of the other is lost (Derrida and Fathy, *Tourner* 88), which amounts to a betrayal of the addressee's singularity. For Magris, too, the structure of great literature aims at an "increase in obscurity, not at clarification" (Magris *Segreti* 12). Yet at a closer look we can perceive the difference between their respective standpoints, which underscores Magris's divergence from poststructuralist positions. Writing for Magris is tantamount to "digging for something that is only revealed (…) during this research" (40). The truth of writing, for Magris, consists precisely of this "something unknown, (…) a secret" (40), which is at once the truth of writing and its devastating potential, because it entails the obligation to know. Magris, in other words, remains anchored to a search for meaning, albeit a controversial, enigmatic one. This is precisely his challenge, his wager against the specter of hollowness and darkness. As he further elaborates in his recently published correspondence with poet Biagio Marin, he believes it is possible to grasp the absolute even within the relativity of our limited human knowledge, which works as a synecdoche, the part for the whole (*Ti devo tanto* 398). Likewise, although consensus can never be affirmed once and for all, it has to be pursued as an ongoing challenge against nothingness. For its part, the secret in Derrida transcends the dialectics of public and private, and cannot be appropriated or shared. Consensus cannot and should not be possible, because the secret has no proper content that can be potentially unlocked, unveiled, and brought to light once and for all. Rather, it amounts to an intrinsic darkness exceeding presence, concealing nothing, hence confirming the bottomless abyss of the signifying mechanism.

In disagreement with this deconstructive approach, Magris upholds the centrality of writing and of literature for the defense of the subject's human dimension and the construction of a common ground. Whereas Derrida denounces the public expression of the secret as "the totalitarianization of democracy" (Derrida *Taste* 59), and hence undermines the illusion of enlightenment associated with a transcendental meaning, for Magris the literary transposition of "the unfathomable mysteries and the (…) passionate darkness" (Magris *Democrazia* 22) of each individual's heart is democratic because it fosters empathy with the lives of others. Where Derrida challenges representational thought as nostalgia for metaphysics and presence, and thus foregrounds the semantic void of *logos*, Magris challenges nothingness and the hollowness of the sign. He supports the ability of *logos*, both as literary word and as law, to probe subjectivity and generate cohesiveness through "a representation of life that is art precisely because it is born of the concrete sense of the individual and of the ability not only to think but also to feel that individuals like us exist, made of flesh and blood and endowed with passions, sentiments, and needs, even though we have never seen them and we are equally unknown to them" (23). Literature hence takes on the quality of Anderson's "imagined community," not as a parochial and exclusive *Heimat* but, rather, as the ongoing construction of a common human experience accounting for the contradictory truths of our individual subjectivity. Magris's secret is not an abyss that swallows meaning and the possibility of sharing. It opens a window onto unknown truths and concealed aspects of our own humanity, which literature aids us to explore.

5.3 The fortress and the drawbridge

Letteratura e ideologia [Literature and Ideology] (2012), which Magris co-authored with Chinese writer and Nobel Prize Winner Gao Xingjian,[9] and *La letteratura è la mia vendetta* [Literature is My Revenge] (2012), co-written with Peruvian writer and Nobel Prize winner Mario Vargas Llosa, are two short meditations on the role of intellectuals and on the centrality of literature as a defense against the power of ideologies. In these works, I argue, the unstable locus of dwelling becomes the terrain of literature itself, which Magris examines as an instance of in-betweenness, a precarious meeting point of individual creativity and an inexhaustible quest for truth.

In *Letteratura e ideologia*, within a wider critique of ideologies like Marxism, nationalism, or liberalism as structures of thought producing dogmatic value systems, Gao Xingjian underlines the need for literature to transcend the granitic rigidity of ideological schemas and to freely express, instead, the individual's feelings and thoughts (*Ideologia* 8). In his view, the power of ideologies has remarkably increased in the last two centuries, whereas in our so-called post-ideological epoch economic interest has replaced ideology and turned it into a mere jumble of empty past discourses (13). Likewise, Magris maintains that even ideology itself becomes a mere arbitrary and groundless opinion whenever intellectuals and writers alike lose that critical consciousness able to overcome visceral immediacy or betray humanity with inhuman abstractions (39). However, Magris brings the discussion one step further, as he clarifies that the Western nineteenth century was a period that, despite the dominance of powerful ideologies, also experienced the remarkable dissent of writers who revolted against the imposition of systems and categories. It is once again the household that provides the figurative semantic context for his claim: the writer, Magris asserts, "is not a responsible father but rather a rebellious son who obeys his demon" (47). Just like the image of the son who, as we have seen in *Utopia e disincanto*, leaves his parents' house and comes back to it only through memories and emotions, here Magris offers another example of domesticity where a protective and confining home has to be trespassed, made open and mobile. This trope further supports Gao Xingjian's attack on the confinement of literature within the constricting domain of ideology, but also warns against what the Chinese writer defines as "the hypertrophism of the 'I'" (14), the excessive expansion and consolidation of identity. The author is not the depository of truth or the savior of the world. It is only by abandoning this strong ideological construction and by returning, instead, to the real and fragile individual, hence recognizing the precariousness and mutability of the self, that it is possible to attain a lucid knowledge of human nature and bear witness to mankind's existential condition.

For Gao Xingjian literature hosts all the individual's feelings and passions; hence, as a sentimental locus, it suggests a connection with the domestic hearth. For Magris, who partly elaborates his previous argument on literature and engagement in *Alfabeti* (477), the writer's moral and political commitment expands the walls of this affective site, rendering it an enlarged household. Although born of a unique, unrepeatable situation, a literary work addresses everyone and "enters in the lives, thoughts, and feelings of the *polis*, of the community" (45). Literature shares with politics the ability to see and soothe not only the needs of single individuals we know but also those of all the people who find themselves in analogous situations "and who are dear to other ones, neither more nor less important than us" (45). As a community builder, literature promotes for Magris an "education to humanity" (50), which occurs instinctively, by *showing* through representation rather than by *preaching*. Extending to the aesthetic realm what he claims from an ethical perspective in *Democrazia, legge e coscienza*, Magris hence redefines democracy as "the fantastic capacity to understand and feel that even the millions of people we do not know—and for whom we cannot obviously nourish personal affection or passion—are no less real and concrete, made of flesh and blood like ourselves and our friends" (46). Literature, Magris had written in *Alfabeti*, "has no duties of ideological coherence, neither messages to propose nor any philosophical and moral systems to enunciate. It can and must represent the contradictory experience of the totality and nothingness of life, of its value and absurdity" (*Alfabeti*

98). Yet, this claim does not intend to challenge the writer's commitment. Although the poetic word in the contemporary West has radically identified with the historical crisis of reason, it has given us a truth which we are able to appropriate only by placing it within a general understanding of the world that needs thought and its connections. Literature hence cannot "be or *directly* become political praxis in its immediacy" (*Quale totalità* 68), because for Magris this would amount to "*using it* instead of receiving its great lesson" (68), which needs to be transposed into our own language.

The message emerging from *Letteratura e ideologia* and *Letteratura è la mia vendetta* poignantly substantiates Mario Vargas Llosa's endorsement of the Triestine author's systematic defense of freedom and of democratic culture. According to Vargas Llosa, Magris does so through a literary activity that practices "politics in its broadest sense, politics that flies high" (*Vendetta* 30) precisely because, rather than directly translating a specific political vision into literature, he ascribes to literature the power to change individuals and reality, making each of us experience the adventurous need to create each time a new world. This engagement, for Vargas Llosa, promotes societies that can be less easily manipulated by power, because reading a great literary work generates critical, independent, freer citizens. The origin of the short volume *La letteratura è la mia vendetta* is an exchange that Magris had with Vargas Llosa on the relationships among the novel, culture, and society at the Peruvian National Library in Lima on December 9, 2009. A conversation between the two writers on the same topics occurred more recently (June 3, 2014), when the University of Florence conferred an honorary degree on Vargas Llosa. Yet we already see them engaged in an implicit dialogue in the edited volume *Il romanzo*, where their respective contributions occupy specular positions and have specular titles. To Vargas Llosa's opening essay "È pensabile il mondo moderno senza il romanzo?" [Is the Modern World Thinkable Without the Novel?], Magris responds with his concluding essay "È pensabile il romanzo senza il mondo moderno?" [Is the Novel Thinkable Without the Modern World?]. Taken together, these two texts synthesize the premises of the more recent, co-written volume, namely, the role of literature as an imaginative enrichment of life and as a promoter of communication and solidarity among people, and the novel as the expression of a totalizing knowledge of the individual that challenges the mutable reality of modernity with its acute awareness of ephemerality and transience.

For Vargas Llosa in *Letteratura è la mia vendetta*, Magris's works provide the best answer to the question "What is the relationship between literature and society" because they delineate a journey that overcomes geographical, cultural, linguistic, and religious barriers separating individuals. Magris's constant search for a common denominator demonstrates that above or beneath those differences there is something that brings us together and allows us to coexist and to communicate (*Vendetta* 22). This something, in Magris, is precisely literature. Anything but a mere escapist realm of signs and images, literature for him offers conceptual, aesthetic, and ethical tools to transcend the barriers of dogmas and stereotypes. It authenticates the affective power of emotions to influence our lives in line with Sarah Ahmed's reinterpretation of emotions in performative terms, that is, as drives that move us, prompting us to act. For Ahmed, "what moves us [and] makes us feel is also that which holds us in place" (Ahmed *Cultural* 11). Emotions connect us to other feeling subjects, as they are simultaneously creators of both individual and collective bodies, and producers of their respective boundaries and interactions (10). This affective communitarian bond generated by literature hence provides a priviledged perspective from which to address what for Magris is *the* contemporary ethico-political problem *par excellence*, namely, the tension between social openness and rejection of otherness (*Vendetta* 56). Confirming and extending to a global scale what he wrote on Europe in *Danube* and *Microcosms*, he highlights how civilization is now threatened by two opposing yet overlapping excesses: the danger of an erasure of all diversities and identities posited by globalization, on the one hand, and, on the other, a reactive and regressive identitarian fever, a visceral self-destructive retreat within one's own peculiarity, which is not lived as a concrete instance of human universality but, rather, as absolute, wild diversity (58).

The protective self-containedness associated with the domestic environment here turns into a suffocating autarchy, insofar as it degrades the household to a self-defensive and simultaneously aggressive enclosure. Magris connotes it as a veritable fortress from which the "regressive culture of diversity and localism, by snarlingly raising the drawbridge, offends not only the larger units of which it is part, but also—(...) above all—itself" (59). Although his critique seems mainly to target a certain miopic European and western tradition, Magris lucidly adds that closure to the influence of values, beliefs, habits, and institutions different from one's own is an attitude we can equally find in the non-European cultural other. Defying a political correctness that, he writes, sometimes turns into pure rhetoric and becomes antidemocratic, he underlines that also foreign communities within the European territory often remain closed in on themselves. Perverting the ethical and aesthetic topos of the open, porous and temporary house, they live in voluntary ghettoes they themselves create, from which they not only keep off European habits and values, but also try to exert pressure on Europe to impose, unconditionally, their own traditions. This disquieting phenomenon prompts Magris to express his dissent and worry at the possible sudden erasure of great conquests of democracy in the name of identity.

Foregrounding once again the need for moderate thinking, Magris here reaffirms identitarian plurality and mobility as the prerequisites for dialogue and for an authentic encounter with others. By the same token, however, mobility should not trespass into anarchic boundlessness. Rather, it has to coexist with a few well-established frontiers able to unconditionally protect some values that we consider definitely acquired, such as equality of rights independently of national, ethnic, sexual, or religious belongings, or the absolute unacceptability of the killing of a child (60–61). These, Magris firmly asserts, are consolidated principles that should no longer constitute topics of negotiations. Whenever they are undermined in intercultural exchange, they justify lifting the drawbridge to defend that ethical space. In such cases, Magris concludes, "the dialogue is closed and the frontier is barred" (61).

The daunting challenge with which Magris's essays confront us is precisely how to preserve the primacy of what both he and Vargas Llosa consider universal values over the more limited national ones, and, simultaneously, how to enact the supposedly true dialogue, founded upon the recognition of multiple kinds of diversity. Although he leaves us at this difficult crossroads, he offers us the support of the most suitable companion to open the way, namely, literature, which, like a drawbridge lowered over the abyss of nothingness, puts us on the road beyond the borders traced by crisis, toward a sense of unity of the human.

Notes

1. Magris has explained his political and institutional vision on other occasions. In *La storia non è finita*, he presents the integration of nations in a federal Europe as an inevitable and liberating process. Federalism in his view can guarantee unity while protecting singular peculiarities. It does not erase authentic patriotism and at the same time opposes resentful secessionism (*Storia* 159). In a debate on Europe with Dutch minister for European Affairs Frans Timmermans, Magris avows that his "European dream is the dream of the centralized European state" ("Debate" 78) with a parliament promulgating laws

"obliging every European citizen" (78) as the problems of each nation are in fact "European problems" (78). This scenario, in his view, would not obliterate the reality of any particular nation or city, because it is not a contradiction to feel at the same time European and part of its components. "I am Triestine, I speak the dialect in Trieste—that is my habit—but I have nothing against the Italian language. I consider myself as Italian, as a citizen of Europe and belonging to the Triestine reality, which I know better than the reality of Sicily or of some other place. I know much better the reality of Italy than the reality of the Netherlands, but it is the same. We must not, we cannot accept this alternative" (72).

2 For an extensive discussion of *habitus* in these terms see Bourdieu, *Logic of Practice* 55–56; *Distinction* 170.

3 Norberto Bobbio (Turin 1909–2004) was a leading Italian political philosopher, who, from a liberal-socialist perspective, strongly defended democracy and peace through the separation and limitation of powers, and endorsed of the rule of law against procedures dictated by pragmatism and convenience. Very critical toward political corruption, he was a regular contributor to the daily newspaper *La Stampa*, and penned numerous important works among which are *Il futuro della democrazia* (1984), *Liberalismo e democrazia* (1985), *L'età dei diritti* (1989).

4 Democracy, Magris claims in *Utopia e disincanto*, "is the daughter of the European tradition" (*Utopia* 258) and constitutes its essence, together with two other founding principles—the primacy of the individual and rationality, which function as guarantees of freedom. In the Preamble to the "Charter of Fundamental Rights of the Union" in the 2004 "Treaty Establishing a Constitution for Europe," the prospective "peaceful future" ("Treaty" 47) to be shared by the peoples of Europe will be founded upon the Union's "spiritual and moral heritage" (47) consisting of "the indivisible, universal values of human dignity, freedom, equality and solidarity" (47). Thanks to "the principles of democracy and the rule of law" (47), the individual is and will be "at the heart of its activities" (47).

5 For a theorization of Italian weak thought see Vattimo and Rovatti, *Weak Thought*; Vattimo *End of Modernity*. Magris has repeatedly distanced himself from the nihilistic conclusions that weak thinkers draw from the assumed implosion of normative principles. See, for instance, "Dal nichilismo" 471–481.

6 For an additional elaboration on the relationships between the law and the universal human values expressed by literature, see Magris "Before the Law."

7 Magris's observations on false democracy have broad implications that transcend the narrow scenario of Italian politics and society. However, even though here Magris does not explicitly refer to any specific person or political group, several of his claims are triggered by the *modus operandi* of former Italian Prime Minister Silvio Berlusconi's government. We can gather this, for instance, from his attack on the avowed intentions of "un nostro presidente del Consiglio" (15)

to appeal to the Italian people against the Constitution, which for Magris is a subversive act that degrades authentic democracy to demagogic management of the status quo.

8   Furthermore, *Segreti e no* closes with an anecdote substantiating the idea that the secret perhaps should not be taken too seriously. It hence diminishes the potential of Magris's overall argumentation, which, in fact, as I have tried to show, has important implications for a wider theoretical debate.

9   Gao Xingjian, born in 1940 in the South-Eastern Chinese city of Ganzhou, was awarded the Nobel Prize for Literature in 2000, to date the only Chinese author who has received it. He is a screenwriter in the absurdist genre (*Signal Alarm* 1982; *Bus Stop* 1983), a novelist (*Soul Mountain* 1990; *One Man's Bible* 1998), a translator (of Beckett and Ionesco) and a painter.

Conclusion

Abstract: *In light of Edward Said and Tony Judt's reflections on the role of the twentieth-century intellectual in the defense and transmission of the leading ideas of his/her time and on the recent disappearance of such a figure, Magris epitomizes the twenty-first-century European intellectual, in the footsteps of figures like Walter Benjamin and George Steiner, but his engagement with literature and values has implications on a global scale.*

Every literary work, independently of its author's ideology, is democratic, according to Magris, because it leads us to identify with other people. The topos of temporary homes in Magris's works allows us to appreciate this creative synergy of private and public, of particular and universal, through which the Italian writer makes a powerful statement about the enduring value of the humanistic tradition as a critical and constructive tool.

Keywords: Edward Said; European intellectuals; George Steiner; humanities; Martha Nussbaum; narrative imagination

Pireddu, Nicoletta. *The Works of Claudio Magris: Temporary Homes, Mobile Identities, European Borders.* New York: Palgrave Macmillan, 2015.
DOI: 10.1057/9781137488046.0009.

places are bobbins, where time is wound up upon itself. To write is to unravel these bobbins, to undo, like Penelope, the fabric of history. (Magris *Microcosms* 214)

In Magris's geography of domesticity—a space that, hosting his memories and hopes, acquires temporal meaning—literary activity takes analysis in its etymological meaning of breaking into pieces. Yet through literature Magris not only unravels but also sews up the texture of reality. He picks up the threads of individual stories and of official history, and weaves messages that defend exceptions and margins against universal falsehoods and sterile abstractions.

Reflecting on the role of the twentieth-century intellectual in the defense and transmission of the leading ideas of his/her time, historian Tony Judt laments the recent disappearance of such a figure (*Reappraisals* 12). For his part, Magris represents to all effects the twenty-first-century European intellectual, in the footsteps of thinkers like Walter Benjamin, Denis de Rougemont, or George Steiner, humanists in the most authentic and broadest sense, and embodiments of a European cultural legacy. One of the most effective syntheses of his personal and poetic profile can be found in the minutes of the Jury that conferred the 2004 Prince of Asturias Award for Letters on him:

> Claudio Magris epitomises the finest humanistic tradition and the pluralism of early twenty-first century European literature in his work—a multifaceted Europe without frontiers, supportive of others and open to dialogue between cultures. Magris employs a powerful narrative voice in his books to highlight certain niches that constitute a land of freedom within which a yearning takes form: European unity within its historical diversity. (Prince of Asturias Foundation Minutes)[1]

"Niches," not spatial totality. "Yearning" rather than mastering. Magris's conquests are never definitive but no less pivotal. His Europe is unfinished, like Bauman's, "a site of continuous experimentation and adventure" (Bauman *Europe* 36) toward human togetherness. While obviously acknowledging "the terrible weight of the past and of history, the deadly power of centuries-old borders of hate and disunity" (*Utopia* 64) and the equally perilous threats undermining the present and the future, both intellectuals concentrate on the answers that Europe can and must continue to give. To be sure, however, the impact of his ideas extends well beyond the borders of the Old Continent. At a moment when, perhaps more dangerously than ever, we are experiencing on a global scale the devastating effects of extremisms and particularisms deriving from the fanaticism of the self, home, and community as spaces of an exclusive *chez soi* defended by insurmountable ideological frontiers, Magris reminds us that nation, homeland, and identity are not "an immobile idol" (*Storia* 159)—they are born, live, and transform themselves.

As Edward Said claims, "intellectuals are *of* their time" (*Representations* 21) and their discourse is informed by a "quite complicated mix between the private and the public worlds" (12) in which personal inflection and sensibility give meaning to the message being articulated for the social world. The representative function of intellectuals lies in their ability to filter the individual and collective history of their time through a novelistic or dramatic lens, which makes their style and performance qualitatively different from those of a merely sociological account, and at the same time ascribes a wider scope to them by universalizing particular experiences. In Magris, the intellectual devoted to public causes coexists with the writer involved in the battle against his own demons (*Vendetta* 12), as he is convinced that "there is no conflict between particularity and universality, between the love of our borders and that of humanity which crosses the border" ("One Language"). Endorsing Dante Alighieri's attachment to his Florentine hometown and river and his simultaneous openness to more extended spaces, he concludes that "our true home is a vaster water; our home (...) is the world, like the sea for the fish" ("One Language"). It is the discovery of this common destiny that, for Magris, authenticates love for one's own dwelling without fetishizing it.

The topos of temporary homes in Magris's works allows us to appreciate precisely this creative synergy of private and public, of particular and universal, through which the Italian writer makes a powerful aesthetic, ethical, and political statement about the enduring value of the humanistic tradition as a critical and constructive tool. Literature offers a mimesis of reality, of its impure and fleeting swarming and its chaotic caducity (*Utopia* 24). Yet mimesis does not mean inert copy. As a believer in hope even in the face of life's most terrible and tragic turns, Magris relies on literature not only as aesthetic education but as an education to humanity founded upon the conviction that reason alone is useless if it does not coexist with the affectivity with which individuals participate in the events of the world.

Every literary work, independently of its author's ideology, is democratic, according to Magris, because "it puts us in other people's clothes and skin" (*Alfabeti* 477; *Vendetta* 46). His works hence authenticate at best Martha Nussbaum's vision of the humanities' pursuit of critical thought, imagination, and empathy toward the variety of human experiences as a guide to democratic citizenship. The cultivation of humanity in the contemporary world, for Nussbaum, requires two fundamental capacities that are also the foundations of Magris's vision: the need to filter our interpersonal relationships through the "narrative imagination" (*Cultivating* 10), that is, the ability to comprehend the world "from the point of view of the other" (10) as the prerequisite for responsible judgments; and the recognition that our "inescapably international" (10) condition requires that we transcend our loyalties to geographic or social localism and that we acknowledge our connection with all other human beings. Magris not only *tells*, but also *shows* us that the power of the humanities lies in their capacity to foster a sympathetic pluralism that sees "the different and foreign not as a threat to be resisted, but as an invitation to explore and understand" (295).

In literature there are many homes, Magris claims, and it is not necessary to choose ideologically among their contrasting voices (*Alfabeti* 13). Magris's own homes teach their dwellers to unmask and stare fearlessly into the void of reality, yet without overlooking the love that surrounds them.

Note

1 In similar terms, the Jury for the 2014 FIL Literary Award in Romance Languages in Guadalajara recognized Magris as a "thinker in various languages" who "embodies the best of the humanist tradition in which he reconciles his own experience with the collective memory of history and the cultures that form part of central Europe, establishing a place for dialog between Mediterranean and Danubian cultures" (Jury "Minutes").

Bibliography

Adorno, Theodor. "Benjamin's *Einbahnstrasse*." *Notes to Literature*. Translated by S. Weber. Vol. 2. New York: Columbia UP, 1992: 322–327.

Agamben, Giorgio. *Language and Death. The Place of Negativity*. Translated by Karen Pinkus. Minneapolis: University of Minnesota Press, 2006.

Ahmed, Sarah. *The Cultural Politics of Emotion*. New York: Routledge, 2004.

Anderson, Benedict. *Imagined Communities*. London: Verso, 1991.

Appadurai, Arjun. *Modernity at Large. Cultural Dimensions of Globalization*. Minneapolis: University of Minnesota Press, 1996.

Appel, Anne Milano. "Plowing Magris's Sea: *Blindly*, with Eyes Open." *Forum Italicum* 40 (2), Fall 2006: 558–571.

Augé, Marc. *Non-places. Introduction to Supermodernity*. London: Verso, 2008.

Bachelard, Gaston. *The Poetics of Space*. Translated by Maria Jolas. Boston: Beacon Press, 1994.

Balibar, Étienne. *Politics and the Other Scene*. Translated by Christine Jones, James Swenson, Chris Turner. London: Verso, 2002.

Barthes, Roland. "The Grain of the Voice" in *Image, Music, Text*. Translated by Stephen Heath. New York: Hill and Wang, 1977.

Bartoloni, Paolo. *On the Cultures of Exile, Translation, and Writing*. West Lafayette: Purdue University Press, 2008.

Bauman, Zygmunt. *Europe. An Unfinished Adventure*. Cambridge: Polity, 2004.

———. *Liquid Life*. Cambridge: Polity, 2005.
———. *Liquid Modernity*. Cambridge: Polity, 2000.
Benjamin, Walter. *Illuminations*. Edited and Introduced by Hannah Arendt. Translated by Harry Zohn. New York: Schocken Books, 1969.
———. *One Way Street and Other Writings*. Translated by Edmund Jephcott and Kingsley Shorter. London: NLB, 1979.
———. *Selected Writings*. Vols 1–4. Edited by M. W. Jennings. Cambridge and London: Bellknap Press of Harvard University Press, 1996–2003.
Bourdieu, Pierre. *Distinction*. Translated by Richard Nice. Cambridge: Harvard University Press, 1984.
———. *The Logic of Practice*. Stanford: Stanford University Press, 1990.
Braidotti, Rosy. *Nomadic Subjects*. New York: Columbia University Press, 1994.
Buck-Morss, Susan. *The Origin of Negative Dialectics*. New York: The Free Press, 1977.
Cassano, Franco. *Southern Thought and Other Essays on the Mediterranean*. Edited and Translated by Norma Bouchard and Valerio Ferme. New York: Fordham University Press, 2012.
Ciccarelli Andrea, "Crossing Borders: Claudio Magris and the Aesthetic of the Other Side." *Journal of European Studies* 42 (4), 2012: 342–361.
Clifford, James. *Routes. Travel and Translation in the Late Twentieth Century*. Cambridge, Mass.: Harvard University Press, 1997.
———. "Traveling Cultures." In Greenberg, Nelson and Treichler eds. *Cultural Studies*. New York: Routledge, 1992: 96–116.
Coda, Elena. "Utopia and Disenchantment in Claudio Magris's *Alla cieca*." *Journal of European Studies* 42 (4), 2012: 375–389.
Cornis Pope, Marcel and John Neubauer eds. *History of the Literary Cultures of East-Central Europe*. Amsterdam: Johns Benjamins, 2010.
Czorycki, Michal. "Figures of Ambiguity. Bucharest and the Black Sea in Claudio Magris, *Danubio*." *The Italianist* 33 (1), 2013: 74–88.
De Certeau, Michel. *The Practice of Everyday Life*. Translated by Steven F. Randall. Berkeley and Los Angeles: University of California Press, 1984.
De Marco, Danilo and G. A. Gonzáles Sanz eds. *Claudio Magris. Argonauta*. Udine: Forum, 2009.
De Rougemont, Denis. *The Meaning of Europe*. Liverpool: Sidgwick and Jackson, 1965.
Deleuze, Gilles and Félix Guattari. "What is a Minor Literature?" Translated by Robert Brinkley. *Mississippi Review* 11 (3), 1983: 13–33.

Derrida, Jacques. *The Other Heading*. Translated by Pascale-Anne Brault and Michael B. Naas. Bloomington: Indiana University Press, 1992.
Derrida, Jacques and Maurizio Ferraris. *A Taste for the Secret*. Translated by Giacomo Donis. Edited by Giacomo Donis and David Webb.
Derrida, Jacques and Safaa Fathy. *Tourner les mots*. Paris: Galilée, 2000.
Dupré, Natalie. *Per un'epica del quotidiano. La frontiera in* Danubio *di Claudio Magris*. Firenze: Cesati, 2009.
Eagleton, Terry. *The Ideology of the Aesthetic*. Oxford: Blackwell, 1990.
European Union. "Treaty Establishing a Constitution for Europe." Luxembourg: Office for Official Publications of the European Communities, 2005.
FIL Literary Award in Romance Languages, "Minutes of the Jury," September 1, 2014. http://www.fil.com.mx/ingles/i_prensa/i_com_muestra_fil.asp?id=1834.
Gilloch, Graeme. *Walter Benjamin. Critical Constellations*. Oxford; Malden, MA: Polity Press; Blackwell, 2002.
Glissant, Édouard. *Poetics of Relation*. Translated by Betsy Wing. Ann Arbor: Michigan University Press, 1997.
Governatori, Licia. *Claudio Magris: l'opera saggistica e narrativa*. Trieste: LINT, 1999.
Habermas, Jürgen. *The Postnational Constellation*. Translated by Max Pensky. Cambridge: Polity, 2001.
——. *The Structural Transformation of the Public Sphere*. Translated by Thomas Burger. Cambridge, Mass.: MIT Press, 1989.
Haine, Scott. "Introduction." In Rittner, Leona, Scott Haine, and Jeffrey Jackson eds. *The Thinking Space. The Café as a Cultural Institution in Paris, Italy and Vienna*. Farnham and Burlington: Ashgate 2013.
Harrison, Thomas. *Essayism. Conrad, Musil, and Pirandello*. Baltimore and London: Johns Hopkins University Press, 1992.
Heidegger, Martin. *Being and Time*. Translated by John Macquarrie and Edward Robinson. New York: Harper and Row, 1962.
——. "Building, Dwelling, Thinking." *Poetry Language Thought*. Translated by Albert Hofstadter. New York: Harper and Row, 1973: 141–160
——. "Letter on Humanism." *Pathmarks*. Edited by William A. McNeill. Cambridge University Press, 1998: 239–275.
——. "What are Poets For?" *Poetry Language Thought*. Translated by Albert Hofstadter. New York: Harper and Row, 1973: 87–139.
Judt, Tony. *Reappraisals*. New York: Penguin, 2008.

Kaminsky, Ann. *Argentina. Stories for a Nation*. Minneapolis: University of Minnesota Press, 2008.

Latham, Jacob Abraham. "The City and the Subject: Benjamin on Language, Materiality, and Subjectivity." *Epoché—The University of California Journal for the Study of Religion* 24, 2006: 49–67.

Magris, Claudio. *A Different Sea*. Translated by M. S. Spurr. London: Harvill, 1993.

——. *Alfabeti. Saggi di letteratura*. Milano: Garzanti, 2008.

——. *Alla cieca*. Milano: Garzanti, 2005.

——. *L'anello di Clarisse*. Torino: Einaudi, 1999.

——. "Before the Law. Literature and Justice." In Claudio Magris. *Literature, Law, and Europe*: 13–27.

——. *Blindly*. Translated by Anne Milano Appel. Toronto: Hamish Hamilton, 2008.

——. "Dal nichilismo al sogno di una nuova innocenza." *L'arte dell'interpretare: studi critici offerti a Giovanni Getto*. Cuneo: Ed. L'Arciere, 1984: 471–481.

——. *Danube*. Translated by Patrick Creagh. New York: Farrar Straus Giroux, 1989.

——. *Danubio*. Milano: Garzanti, 1999.

——. "Danubio e post-Danubio." *Rivista di studi ungheresi* 7, 1992: 21–32.

——. "È pensabile il romanzo senza il mondo moderno?" In Franco Moretti ed. *Il romanzo* Vol. I. Torino: Einaudi, 2001: 869–880.

——. *Fra il Danubio e il mare. Il mondo di Claudio Magris*. Edited by Francesco Conversano e Nene Grignaffini. Milano: Garzanti, 2011.

——. "Identità ovvero incertezza." *Lettere italiane* 55 (4), 2003: 519–527.

——. *Il Conde*. Genova: Il Melangolo, 1993.

——. "Il mio romanzo goriziano." *Studi goriziani* 74, July–December 1991: 27–37.

——. *Il mito absburgico nella letteratura austriaca moderna*. Torino: Einaudi, 1996.

——. *Illazioni su una sciabola*. Milano: Garzanti, 1992.

——. *Inferences from a Sabre*. Translated by Mark Thompson. New York: George Braziller, 1990.

——. *Itaca e oltre*. Milano: Garzanti, 1999.

——. *La mostra*. Milano: Garzanti, 2001.

——. *La storia non è finita*. Milano: Garzanti, 2006.

——. "La terza alba della Mitteleuropa". *Corriere della sera*, April 9, 2013: 39.

——. *Le voci*. Genova: Il Melangolo, 1995.

——. *Lei dunque capirà*. Milano: Garzanti, 2006.
——. "Limes. Frontiera dell'essere, cerchio che racchiude." *Palomar* 1, 1992: 51–72.
——. *L'infinito viaggiare*. Milano: Mondadori, 2005.
——. *Literature, Law, and Europe. The First Romano Guarnieri Lecture in Italian Studies and a Debate with Frans Timmermans*. Edited by Harald Hendrix. *Italianistica Ultraiectina*, 5. Utrecht: Igitur, Utrecht Publishing and Archiving Services, 2009.
——. *Livelli di guardia*. Milano: Garzanti, 2011.
——. *Lontano da dove*. Torino: Einaudi, 1989.
——. *Microcosmi*. Milano: Garzanti, 1999.
——. *Microcosms*. Translated by Iain Halliday. London: Harvill, 1999.
——. "Mitteleuropa: Reality and Myth of a Word." *Edinburgh Review*, 87, Winter 1991–1992: 141–153.
——. "Narrating History, Inventing History: The Making of *Blindly*." *Journal of European Studies* 42 (4), 2012: 324–332.
——. "One Language, Many Cultures." *Almost Island*, Winter 2012: 1–3.
——. "Personaggi dalla biografia imperfetta," in *Gli spazi della diversità. Atti del convegno internazionale "Rinnovamento del codice narrativo in Italia dal 1945 al 1992*. Vol. II. Roma: Bulzoni; Leuven: Leuven University Press: 617–632.
——. *Quale totalità. Dibattito con Antonio Villani, Marino Freschi e Carlo Sini*. Napoli: Guida, 1985.
——. *Segreti e no*. Milano: Bompiani, 2014.
——. *Stadelmann*. Milano: Garzanti, 1988.
——. *Stadelmann* in *Voices. Three Plays*. Translated by Paul Vangelisti. Los Angeles: Green Integer, 2007: 17–114.
——. "The Fair of Tolerance." Amsterdam: Praemium Erasmianum Essay, 2001. http://www.eurozine.com/articles/article_2001-12-27-magris-en.html.
——."The Self that Writes." http://almostisland.com/archives/2008-monsoon/claudio_magris.php.
——. *Ti devo tanto di ciò che sono. Carteggio con Biagio Marin*. Milano: Garzanti, 2014.
——. "Trieste," in "Le città dell'Orient Express." Edited by Cin Calabi. *Atlante*, May 1982: 50–61.
——. *To Have Been* in *Voices. Three Plays*. Translated by Paul Vangelisti. Los Angeles: Green Integer, 2007: 7–11.
——. *Un altro mare*. Milano: Garzanti, 2003.

——. *Utopia e disincanto*. Milano: Garzanti, 2001.
——. *Voices* in *Voices. Three Plays*. Translated by Paul Vangelisti. Los Angeles: Green Integer, 2007: 115–140.
——. "You Will Therefore Understand." Translated by Anne Milano Appel. *Quaderni d'italianistica* XXXII (1), 2001: 7–25.
Magris, Claudio and Marco Alloni. *La vita non è innocente. Dialogo con Claudio Magris*. Lugano: ADV Publishing, 2008.
Magris, Claudio and Angelo Ara. *Trieste. Un'identità di frontiera*. Torino: Einaudi, 1982.
Magris, Claudio and Andrea Ciccarelli. "Sette domande a Claudio Magris." *Italica* 81 (3), 2004: 402–423.
Magris, Claudio and Fabio Gambaro "Entretien. Claudio Magris 'Je suis un écrivain de frontière.'" *Magazine Littéraire* 370, 1998: 98–103.
Magris, Claudio and Stefano Levi Della Torre. *Democrazia, legge e coscienza*. Torino: Codice, 2010.
Magris, Claudio and Sandra Parmegiani. "A colloquio con Claudio Magris. Tra approdi e naufragi dell'Io: considerazioni su vent'anni di narrativa." *Italian Culture* 22, 2004: 137–156.
Magris, Claudio and Frans Timmermans. "Debate on Europe." In Claudio Magris. *Literature, Law, and Europe*: 59–80.
Magris, Claudio and Gao Xinjian. *Letteratura e ideologia*. Milano: Bompiani, 2012.
Magris, Claudio and Giulio Zucchini. "When Europe is One State." [http://www.cafébabel.co.uk/article/19469/claudio-magris-when-europe-is-one-state.html].
Magris, Claudio and Hans Ulrich Obrist. "Hans Ulrich Obrist Interviews Claudio Magris," *European Alternatives* 2008. http://www.euroalter.com/2008/hans-ulrich-obrist-interviews-claudio-magris/.
Magris, Claudio and Mario Vargas Llosa. *La letteratura è la mia vendetta*. Milano: Mondadori, 2012.
Magris, Claudio and Rosa Maria Rinaldi. "Claudio Magris." *Domus* 658, February 1985: 52–53.
Marchand, Laurent. "Lire Claudio Magris": la Mitteleuropa, antidote pour une Europe en crise." [http://international.blogs.ouest-france.fr/archive/2013/04/10/magris-mitteleuropa-europe-crise-globalisation-litterature-n.html].
Matvejević, Predrag. *Il Mediterraneo e l'Europa*. Milano: Garzanti, 1998.
Mazzini, Giuseppe. "D'una letteratura europea." *D'una letteratura europea e altri saggi*. Fasano: Schena, 1991: 27–75.

Michelstaedter, Carlo. *La persuasione e la rettorica*. Edited by Sergio Campailla. Milano: Adelphi 1999.
Moretti, Franco ed. *Il romanzo* Vol. I. Torino: Einaudi, 2001.
Nancy, Jean-Luc. *La création du monde ou la mondialisation*. Paris: Galilée, 2002.
——. *The Creation of the World or Globalization*. Translated by F. Raffoul and D. Pettigrew. Albany: SUNY Press, 2007.
——. Nietzsche, Friedrich. *The Gay Science*. Translated by Walter Kaufmann. New York: Vintage, 1974.
Nussbaum, Martha. *Cultivating Humanity*. Cambridge: Harvard University Press, 1997.
Oldenburg, Ray. *The Great Good Place*. New York: Marlowe, 1989.
Parmegiani, Sandra. "The Presence of Myth in Magris's Postmillennial Narrative." *Quaderni d'italianistica* 32 (1), 2011: 111–134.
Pellegrini, Ernestina. *Epica sull'acqua. L'opera letteraria di Claudio Magris*. Bergamo: Moretti & Vitali, 1997.
——. "Claudio Magris o dell'identità plurale." In Claudio Magris, *Opere*. Vol. I. Edited by Ernestina Pellegrini. Milano: I Meridiani, Mondadori, 2012: xi–lxx.
Pireddu, Nicoletta. "European Ulyssiads: Claudio Magris, Milan Kundera, Eric-Emmanuel Schmitt," *Comparative Literature*, Special Issue "Odyssey, Exile, Return," eds M. Zerba and A. Russo, 67 (3), Summer 2015.
——. "On the Threshold, Always Homeward Bound: Claudio Magris's European Journey." *Journal of European Studies* 42 (4), 2012, Special Issue "Claudio Magris and European identity," ed. Sandra Parmegiani: 333–341.
Prince of Asturias Foundation, Minutes of the Jury. [(http://www.fpa.es/en/prince-of-asturias- awards/awards/2004-claudio-magris.html?texto=acta&especifica=0].
Said, Edward. Response to "What is Patriotism?" *The Nation*, 253 (3), July 15–22, 1991: 116.
——. *Representations of the Intellectual: The 1993 Reith Lectures*. New York: Pantheon, 1994.
Schächter, Elizabeth. *Origin and Identity: Essays on Svevo and Trieste*. Leeds: Northern Universities Press, 2000.
Slataper, Scipio. *Scritti politici*. Roma: Alberto Stock, 1925.
Sontag, Susan. "Introduction." In Walter Benjamin, *One Way Street and Other Writings*. Translated by Edmund Jephcott and Kingsley Shorter. London: NLB, 1979: 7–28.

Steiner, George. *The Idea of Europe*. Tilburg: Nexus Institute, 2004.
Stevens, Paul and Robert Hardwick Weston. "Free Time." *Social Text* 94, 26 (1), 2008: 137–164.
Trentini, Daria. "L'idea di Mitteleuropa nell'opera di Claudio Magris." *Il Veltro* 46 (5–6) 2002: 539–553.
Tuan, Yu-Fu. *Space and Place. The Perspective of Experience*. Minneapolis: University of Minnesota Press, 1977.
——. *Topophilia*. Englewood Cliffs: Prentice Hall, 1974.
Vargas Llosa, Mario. "È pensabile il mondo moderno senza il romanzo?" in Franco Moretti ed. *Il romanzo* vol. I. Torino: Einaudi, 2001: 3–15.
Vattimo, Gianni. *The End of Modernity*. Baltimore: Johns Hopkins University Press, 1988.
Vattimo, Gianni and Pier Aldo Rovatti. *Weak Thought*. Albany: State University of New York Press, 2012.

Index

abode
 temporary. *See* home
Adorno, Theodor, 78, 99, 100
Adriatic. *See* sea
Agamben, Giorgio, 23
Ahmed, Sarah, 118
Alcestis, 41
Alighieri, Dante, 125
Alloni, Marco, 108, 111
Anderson, Benedict, 46, 55, 116
Antigone, 111
Appadurai, Arjun, 80
Ara, Angelo, 35, 40, 49
Ariadne, 99
Augé, Marc, 95

Bachelard, Gaston, 5, 7, 11–15, 19, 20, 29, 30, 41, 44, 95
Balibar, Étienne, 92, 97, 104
Barthes, Roland, 23
Bartoloni, Paolo, 31
Baudelaire, Charles, 29, 40, 78
Bauman, Zygmunt, 47, 64–66, 69–70, 106, 124
Beethoven, Ludwig van, 61
Benjamin, Walter, 3, 77–81, 99, 100, 124
Bhabha, Homi, 8
Birken, Sigmund von, 59
Bobbio, Norberto, 108, 121

border, 6, 20, 26, 33, 44, 52, 62, 66, 68, 72, 74, 85–88, 90–91, 95, 97, 103, 104, 125
 and citizen, 97
Bourdieu, Pierre, 121
Braidotti, Rosi, 8
Broch, Herman, 67
Büchner, Georg, 2
Budapest, 2, 53, 71

café, 36, 49, 61, 71, 80–85
 Caffè delle Giubbe Rosse, 82
 Caffè Florian, 81
 Caffè Greco, 82
 Caffè San Marco, 34, 44, 77, 81–84, 87
Canary Islands, 52
Carnia, 43, 44, 46
Casanova, Giacomo, 81
Cassano, Franco, 62, 108
Céline, Louis Ferdinand, 60
Ciccarelli, Andrea, 3, 4, 49, 74, 103
Cioran, Emil, 67
civility, 106
Clifford, James, 40, 103
Coda, Elena, 4
coffeehouse, 80, 83, 89. *See* café
Cratylus, 17
Creon, 111

D'Annunzio, Gabriele, 82

Index

De Certeau, Michel, 5, 6, 36, 41, 62, 72, 80
De Musset, Alfred, 47
Deleuze, Gilles, 70
democracy, 84, 109
 and literature, 117
Derrida, Jacques, 104–105, 113–115
disenchantment, 2, 4, 7, 55, 61, 68, 82, 84, 90
domesticity. *See* home
Dostoevsky, Fyodor, 38, 109, 110
Dupré, Natalie, 5, 49
dwelling. *See* home

emotions
 and mobility, 118
Europe, 7–8, 16, 33, 38, 52–56, 61–63, 68–77, 83–88, 91, 93, 96, 99, 103–107, 118, 120–121, 124
 European intellectual, 124
Eurydice, 20, 21, 22
exile, 12, 94

fluidity, 5, 14, 16, 20, 28, 30, 57, 61, 65
freedom
 and liberal thinking, 107
Freud, Sigmund, 38, 92
frontier, 5, 26, 33, 39, 62, 72, 75, 85–88, 97, 105, 120. *See* border
fundamentalism
 and secularism, 108

Gambaro, Fabio, 56
Glissant, Édouard, 103, 114
globalization, 91, 103, 104, 118
Goethe, Johann Wolfgang von, 12–17, 61
Goldoni, Carlo, 81
Goli Otok, 91–93, 95, 101
Governatori, Licia, 9
Grado, 85, 88
Grillparzer, Franz, 2
Guattari, Félix, 70

Habermas, Jürgen, 55, 83
habitat, 66, 82, 88, 96, 106, 107

habitus, 106, 107, 121
Haine, Scott, 81, 82
Harrison, Thomas, 107
Heidegger, Martin, 21, 22, 31, 59, 60, 69
Heraclitus, 17
history, 4, 28, 33, 37, 43, 53, 62, 71, 86, 88, 91, 92, 96, 98, 99, 112, 124
Hölderlin, Friedrich, 63, 71
home, 2, 3, 5–8, 11–23, 26, 28–30, 33–35, 37–49, 52, 57, 60, 61, 65, 66, 73, 74, 79–90, 94–99, 103, 105–106, 112, 113, 117, 124, 125
 temporary home and city, 34
homeland, 5, 6, 8, 16, 33–37, 42–44, 46–48, 59, 69, 73, 88, 90, 96, 99, 103, 105, 125
house. *See* home
household. *See* home
humanities
 and pluralism, 8, 126

Ibsen, Henrik, 2
identity, 4, 6–8, 11–18, 22, 28, 30, 33, 36–43, 46–48, 52–57, 60, 64–70, 73–75, 80, 86–92, 95–96, 99, 103–106, 113, 114, 117, 120, 125
inhabiting
 in Heidegger, 21

Jameson, Fredric, 40
Jorgensen, Jorgen, 93–96
journey, 11, 12, 15, 24, 33, 37, 40, 52, 57–59, 62, 64–65, 71, 73, 77, 81, 89–91, 95–96, 111–112, 118. *See* travel
Joyce, James, 36, 85
Judt, Tony, 124

Kafka, Franz, 70, 112
Kaminsky, Ann, 25
Kant, Immanuel, 109
Kleist, Bernd Heinrich Wilhelm von, 2
Krasnov, Peter, 42–43, 45–48, 59

Levi, Carlo, 82
Levi della Torre, Stefano, 111

liquidity, 4, 5, 29, 57, 64, 65, 88
literature, 3, 6, 8, 12, 17, 36, 53, 55, 58, 74, 81, 83, 100, 105, 115–120, 124–126
location. *See* space
Lukács, Georg, 107
Lyotard, Jean-François, 4

Magris, Claudio
   Alfabeti, 2, 7, 117, 125, 126
   Alla cieca. See Blindly
   Blindly, 2, 9, 48, 73, 86, 90–101, 105
   Danube, 2, 3, 5, 11, 31, 48, 57–69, 74–75, 77, 81, 97–98, 103, 107, 118, 128
   Danubio. See Danube
   Democrazia, legge e coscienza, 107, 108, 111, 115, 117
   A Different Sea, 11, 24, 27, 101
   Essere già stati. See To Have Been
   "The Fair of Tolerance", 68, 104
   "Identità uguale incertezza", 17, 95
   Il Conde, 24, 28, 29, 30
   "Il mio romanzo goriziano", 28
   Il mito absburgico nella letteratura austriaca moderna, 2, 52
   Illazioni su una sciabola. See Inferences from a Sabre
   Inferences From a Sabre, 42–48, 59
   Itaca e oltre, 11, 36, 37
   L'anello di Clarisse, 54, 57
   L'infinito viaggiare, 2, 18, 74, 97
   La mostra, 39, 40, 50
   La storia non è finita, 4, 75, 107, 109, 110, 120
   La vita non è innocente, 7, 73, 101, 107, 108, 111, 112
   Le voci. See Voices
   Lei dunque capirà. See You Will Therefore Understand
   Livelli di guardia, 107, 108, 109
   Lontano da dove, 2, 12, 48, 74
   Microcosmi. See Microcosms
   Microcosms, 2, 39, 48, 49, 73, 77–93, 95, 97, 98, 100, 101, 103, 118, 124
   "Mitteleuropa: Reality and Myth of a Word", 53
   "Personaggi dalla biografia imperfetta", 18, 25, 27
   Segreti e no, 2, 108, 113, 122
   Stadelmann, 2, 11–18
   Ti devo tanto di ciò che sono, 115
   To Have Been, 74
   Trieste. Un'identità di frontiera, 35
   Un altro mare. See A Different Sea
   Utopia e disincanto, 2, 7, 17, 18, 34, 39, 55, 72, 82, 88, 110, 112, 117, 121
   You Will Therefore Understand, 2, 18–22, 30, 31, 34, 90
Magris, Claudio and Gao Xingjian
   Letteratura e ideologia, 116, 118
Magris, Claudio and Mario Vargas Llosa
   La letteratura è la mia vendetta, 99, 116, 118
Marin, Biagio, 115
Matvejević, Predrag, 28
Mazzini, Giuseppe, 55
Mediterranean. *See* sea
Michelstaedter, Carlo, 24, 25
Mináč, Vladimir, 70
Mitteleuropa, 38, 52–57, 73–74, 85–86, 89, 97, 100
mobility, 6, 8, 18, 29, 30, 35, 44, 62, 64, 65, 89, 91, 97, 114, 120
Montaigne, Michel de, 107
morality. *See* values
Mreule, Enrico, 11, 24, 30
Musil, Robert, 35, 53
Mussolini, Benito, 87

Nancy, Jean-Luc, 91, 99
nation, 7, 8, 33, 46, 53, 63, 70, 92, 99, 125
region, 86
Nietzsche, Friedrich, 5, 38, 103
Nussbaum, Martha, 125, 126

Obrist, Hans Ulrich, 6, 7, 34, 54
odyssey. *See* Ulysses

Oldenburg, Ray, 83, 84
Orpheus, 20, 21, 22

Parmegiani, Sandra, 4, 7, 101
Pellegrini, Ernestina, 5, 9, 27
Pireddu, Nicoletta, 58
place, 5, 6, 8, 14, 20, 25–26, 29, 34, 36–38, 40–43, 46, 48, 52, 60, 78–83, 86, 89, 93, 95, 100–101, 106, 113, 118
politics, 55
    Italian, 109
postmodernism, 4, 110
precariousness, 4, 12, 17, 24, 30, 35, 37, 56, 59, 64, 74, 80, 89, 90, 94, 105, 113, 117
Pressburger, Giorgio, 31
Proust, Marcel, 3, 77

relocation, 95. *See* mobility
Rinaldi, Rosa Maria, 34
Robert, Reiter, 35, 68
Roth, Joseph, 48, 53, 61
Rougemont, Denis de, 84, 124

Sábato, Ernesto, 7
Said, Edward, 8, 125
Schächter, Elizabeth, 49
Schnitzler, Arthur, 2
Schopenhauer, Arthur, 27, 38, 82
sea, 4, 5, 19, 25, 28–30, 34, 41, 44, 50, 64, 67, 73, 81, 83, 86, 88, 97–98, 103, 125
Sennet, Richard, 106
Slataper, Scipio, 36, 38, 53
Sofianopulo, Cesare, 40, 50
Sontag, Susan, 78, 79, 100
Sophocles, 111
space, 2, 5–7, 11–15, 17, 20–27, 36–42, 44, 46–47, 59, 62, 72–74, 77, 78, 80, 81, 84, 89, 90, 95–98, 100, 104, 106, 113, 114, 120, 124
Stadelmann, Johann Carl Wilhelm, 11–18, 22, 30, 39
Steiner, George, 84, 124

Stendhal (Marie-Henri Beyle), 82
Stifter, Adalbert, 61
Svevo, Italo, 36

temporality, 15, 17, 27, 40, 45, 64, 94
threshold, 19, 22, 28, 34, 44, 62, 66, 79, 85, 105, 108, 112
Timmel, Vito, 39–42, 49, 50
Tito, Josip Broz, 27, 91, 92, 93
tolerance, 59, 68, 104, 105, 108
Tommasini, Muzio de', 85
totality, 3, 18, 21, 34, 37, 53, 61, 68, 91, 110, 114, 117, 124
transience. *See* temporality
travel, 2, 5, 12, 27, 48, 58, 59, 90, 97. *See* journey
Trieste, 3, 31–43, 49, 53, 77, 82–85, 89, 92, 94, 100
Tuan, Yu-Fu, 5, 7, 12, 38, 46, 54, 89, 90, 95, 96, 107, 113
Turin, 34, 83, 121
Tyrol, 86, 87

Ulysses, 11, 12, 30, 48
Urzidil, Johannes, 53
utopia, 4, 7, 55

values, 3, 6, 8, 26, 35, 61, 67, 69, 86, 104–106, 109, 110–112, 119–121
Vargas Llosa, Mario, 116, 118, 120
Vattimo, Gianni, 121
Vegliani, Franco, 49
Vienna, 49, 53, 61, 67, 83

Wagner, Richard, 81
weak thought, 110, 121
Weber, Max, 108, 110
Weininger, Otto, 61
Werfel, Franz, 53
Willemer, Marianne Jung, 61
Wittgenstein, Ludwig, 61, 74

Xingjian, Gao, 116, 117, 122

Zucchini, Giulio, 104

GPSR Compliance
The European Union's (EU) General Product Safety Regulation (GPSR) is a set
of rules that requires consumer products to be safe and our obligations to
ensure this.

If you have any concerns about our products, you can contact us on

ProductSafety@springernature.com

In case Publisher is established outside the EU, the EU authorized
representative is:

Springer Nature Customer Service Center GmbH
Europaplatz 3
69115 Heidelberg, Germany

www.ingramcontent.com/pod-product-compliance
Lightning Source LLC
LaVergne TN
LVHW041955060526
838200LV00002B/32